1848 was the Ye[...] [...]w
the tiny Grand D[...] [...]r
aftermath. Prin[...] [...]e
Grand Duke, na[...] [...]r
parents are ass[...] [...]er
cousin Prince Franz Johann. But she is bewildered and
terrified when he refuses to acknowledge that the ragged
waif before him is indeed the Princess. He insists that
the real Anna lies in her coffin and forces her to marry
his mysterious prisoner Prince Stephan. How can Anna
convince this enigmatic man—a revolutionary leader
—that she is really the Princess?

THE
PRINCESS

JASMINE CRESSWELL

MILLS & BOON LIMITED
London · Sydney · Toronto

First published in Great Britain 1982 by
Robert Hale Limited, Clerkenwell House,
Clerkenwell Green, London EC1R 0HT

© Jasmine Cresswell 1982

Australian copyright 1984
Philippine copyright 1984

This edition published 1984 by
Mills & Boon Limited, 15–16 Brook's Mews,
London W1A 1DR

ISBN 0 263 74618 6

Set in 11/11½pt Linotron Times
04/0484

Photoset by Rowland Phototypesetting Limited,
Bury St Edmunds, Suffolk
Made and printed in Great Britain by
Cox and Wyman Limited, Reading

For Fiona, Vanessa and Sarah,
with love.

CHAPTER
ONE

PRINCE Franz Johann nodded to the guards who surrounded him and ordered one of the soldiers to unbar the iron door to the cell. The fetid air rushed out, making the Prince gag. 'Lights!' he commanded sharply.

A soldier touched his taper to the oil-lamp hung on the wall by the door, and the interior of the cell was illuminated by a flickering yellow glow. Even in that smoky light, it was possible to see that the cell walls seeped with moisture and the only brightness came from a vivid green fungus growing in patches over the stone floor.

Straw rustled, and the Prince's eyes fixed with reluctant fascination on the tall, pale figure which rose from the dirty straw pallet pushed into one corner of the cell. The man spoke.

'Why, little brother, I am honoured. You have come to call *again*.'

At the sound of the mocking voice, Prince Franz Johann's pallid complexion faded to a sickly hue of grey. 'Tell me where you have hidden the papers and you shall go free,' he said harshly.

The man laughed softly. 'Come, little brother, you cannot expect me to believe such an unlikely promise. I should be dead within five minutes of the papers being in your hands.'

'You have my word that you will go free,' the Prince said.

The prisoner laughed again. The quiet, mocking sound echoed against the stone walls, then faded into silence. He did not bother to make any other reply to the Prince's offer.

'Damn you! I shall have those names and my father's mad scrawlings if you rot here for ever!'

The man shrugged. 'We shall see . . . little brother.'

'Don't call me that!'

'Am I inaccurate?'

'You are the younger, not I! You are not even my true brother.'

The prisoner bowed. 'I beg your pardon, Your Highness.' The over-polite words were a subtle insult of their own.

'Chain him up!' the Prince screamed to the guards.

He watched with satisfaction as one of the soldiers locked the iron cuffs over the prisoner's wrists. 'You have seven days to change your mind,' the Prince said, his voice once again under control. 'My patience will last no longer, I warn you.'

'My dear little brother . . .' The taunting voice paused. 'Unless Your Highness improves the cuisine in this noble establishment, I fear you may be deprived of the supreme pleasure of ordering my execution.'

Prince Franz Johann snatched a torch from one of the guards and held it high. The man closed his eyes against the unexpectedly bright light, which revealed a face gaunt with malnutrition. His skin, visible through the tatters of his shirt, was bruised and bleeding from unhealed wounds.

The Prince turned away. 'Give him food!' He flung out the command and thrust the torch into the hands of a waiting guard.

'What are you waiting for?' he yelled at the captain. 'Can't you see that I'm ready to leave?'

The soldiers reformed themselves into a guard of honour. The cell door clanged shut. The prisoner was once again alone in the darkness.

CHAPTER
TWO

THE Dowager Grand Duchess of Carthia inspected Anna Teresa's appearance with a steady gaze.

'You may sit down,' the Dowager said. Her voice sounded cool and controlled, but she turned her head abruptly and stared out of the arched castle windows so that she could conceal the hint of sympathy which had crept into her eyes.

'You look charming, my dear Anna,' she said as her granddaughter sat gracefully on the edge of a small, gilded chair. 'Your new ballgown is delightful. Your mother has exquisite taste in clothes.'

'I'm pleased that you approve. It wouldn't do to offend the eyes of the Austrian generals.' Princess Anna Teresa, elder daughter of the reigning Grand Duke of Carthia, made no effort to disguise her sarcasm. She tapped her satin-shod foot impatiently, biting her lower lip as she waited for the Dowager to speak. After a few moments of silence, she sprang up from the chair, unable to tolerate the enforced inactivity.

'Please ask Papa if I may be excused from attending the ball, Grandmother. You know how much I hate the Austrians and their wretched Imperial army! I shall never understand why my father called in Austrian troops to control Carthian peasants and a few hot-headed students from the

University. How could he appeal to the Hapsburgs, of all people?'

The Dowager drew in a sharp breath. 'Do not speak foolishly, child, when you are blessed with a considerable supply of intelligence. Learn to use your wits before you speak, instead of afterwards. The Austrian troops were summoned to crush a rebellion against your father's rule. Without their aid, Carthia would by now be a republic. Did you wish 1848 to go down in history as the last year of rule by your family? After four hundred years? Did you wish to follow King Ludwig of Bavaria, forced into exile, just because you resent the fact that your father needed help from the Austrian Emperor?'

'I don't believe the peasants would have forced my father to abdicate. Surely they love him.'

The Dowager's laughter was entirely cynical. She lifted her shoulders in a faint shrug that spoke clearly of her French origins. 'Oh yes! The peasants love your father: just as much as the Paris mob loved King Louis of France. They love him just as much as the peasants on my French estates loved my father when they betrayed him to the Committee of Public Safety and condemned him to the embrace of Madame Guillotine. There can never be true affection between those who rule and those who are ruled, my child. The most we can hope for is the occasional shared interest in repelling a foreign aggressor.'

'The English love Queen Victoria. My governess told me so.'

'Your governess was a silly English spinster, and she has as great a deal to answer for,' the Dowager said grimly. 'She stuffed your head full of romantic nonsense about the nobility of political democracy and then died of influenza before she had to deal with the consequences of your wrong ideas. Instead of wasting my time discussing Queen Victoria and her loving British subjects, I shall take this opportunity to remind you that your father will be announcing your betrothal tonight. You cannot avoid the ball.'

'Why can't my father announce the betrothal next week, after the Austrians have gone?'

The Dowager avoided her granddaughter's gaze. 'Your parents want to be sure that the Austrians carry word of it back to the Emperor. Once *he* has approved the match, it cannot be set aside for any reason.'

'It's bad enough that I have to marry my cousin,' the Princess exclaimed bitterly. 'It's even worse that I have to sit beside him all night and look as though I'm enjoying it! His Serene Highness, Prince Franz Johann, heir to the Grand Duchy of Carthia, Count of Styria, Count of Innesbad, and Baron of Bruchwald.' She whirled passionately around the room, her skirts swirling up to reveal elegant silk-clad ankles and an indiscreet six inches of lace petticoat. 'He is a toad,' she said fiercely.

The Dowager made no effort to defend her grandson. She merely lifted her shoulders in another exquisite shrug. 'He is, however, the toad whom you must marry.'

'Why *me*?' Princess Anna Teresa possessed a magnificent pair of dark eyes. When she was angry they sparkled with the hidden fires of a sapphire and at the moment they flashed with brilliant blue flames. It was fortunate, thought her grandmother dispassionately, that there was no susceptible young man around to observe her.

'Why me?' the Princess repeated. 'Why not my sister Luisa?'

'Franz Johann prefers to marry you,' replied the Dowager, and her gaze once more flickered somewhat evasively towards the castle window.

'But Luisa wants to marry Franz. She would like to be the next Grand Duchess of Carthia and she doesn't mind if Franz is an inevitable part of the bargain.'

There was a slight pause before the Dowager spoke again. 'Franz Johann naturally prefers to marry you. You are the elder daughter. Your father has decided, for various reasons, to comply with your cousin's wishes. Franz Johann helped your father crush the revolution, and your marriage will unite the two greatest Carthian families as well as the western and eastern regions of the country. Your dowry is greater than Luisa's, my dear.'

Princess Anna Teresa sat down abruptly on the gilded chair, concealing a shudder with some difficulty. 'So I am to be the prize for Franz Johann's loyal service to my father during the revolution. Oh why did I have to be older than Luisa? There is so much else I want to do before I must marry!' She did not wait for her grandmother to respond to these pointless remarks. She stared at her hands, her voice shaking with revulsion. 'I cannot bear the thought that I must be the mother to Franz Johann's children. His eyes bulge and his hands sweat.'

'I have never tried to say that Prince Franz Johann is an attractive suitor,' the Dowager said calmly. 'I merely pointed out that it is your inescapable duty to marry him.' Her glance softened as it rested upon the smooth chestnut gleam of her granddaughter's head. 'Tolerate him for a few years, Anna Teresa. Give him two or three children and then you may find yourself as handsome a lover as you wish. When you have produced two sons, I will take you to Paris myself, and there you will discover what it means to love and be loved with true passion.'

Anna shuddered slightly. 'I don't want a lover, Grandmother,' she said with a hint of despair. 'I just want to like my husband a little bit. I don't even expect to fall madly in love with him.' She crossed the room hurriedly and knelt at her grandmother's side. 'I can't bear it when my cousin touches me,' she confided. 'Last night, when Papa agreed to our betrothal, Franz Johann kissed me. It was like being kissed by a dead codfish. Cold and slimy.'

'He may look like a toad and kiss like a cod, but he is a clever man and our duchy has need of his unique skills. Your father certainly could not govern without his support and you are old enough to learn that fact now.' The Dowager rose to her feet and walked imperiously to one side of the huge marble fireplace. 'I have allowed you to talk a great deal of nonsense to me, my dear, because you are my favourite grandchild. Heaven knows why, since you are stubborn and romantic, which is a fatal combination. But no more nonsense. I shall simply remind you of your duty and your obligations to the people of Carthia. You do not have to enjoy your cousin's embraces, Anna. You have merely to endure them. It is a small price to pay for the security of your country.'

'I will marry anybody else,' the Princess said desperately. 'I will marry Count Otto, or my cousin

Bertram even though he is more than forty.'

'Prince Franz Johann has already made a formal offer and, as you know very well, your father accepted it last night.'

'Cousin Franz doesn't like me for myself. He only wants me because of my dowry and because I am the elder daughter of the Grand Duke.'

The Dowager Grand Duchess raised one eyebrow in supercilious and devastating enquiry. 'Why else should he want you save for your dowry and the fact of your royal birth? Franz Johann is a worthy heir to the dukedom. He is prepared to sacrifice his personal preferences in the interest of making the most expedient marriage for his country. Would you wish him to desire you for your physical attractions?' The Dowager ignored Anna's heightened colour and continued ruthlessly. 'Be thankful that his visits to your bedroom will be made as a duty, not as a pleasure. His tastes, so my spies tell me, are rather exotic.'

'Please, Grandmother . . . Help me.'

'I am helping you. Accept the fact that you will marry your cousin, Prince Franz Johann of Innesbad. I have nothing more to say upon the matter.'

The Grand Duke Frederick of Carthia stood in the centre of the Small Salon, a vaulted chamber badly misnamed since it was not an inch less than forty feet long and well over fifteen feet high. The Duke's shoulders slumped with fatigue, Anna noticed, but his lined face looked more relaxed than it had for months.

Compassion surged within her, compassion tinged with guilt. She hardly knew her father, having seen him only on state occasions since she left the schoolroom, and almost never before her fifteenth birthday. But she knew that the last two years had been hard for him, as they had been for all the other princes in Central Europe. He had finally crushed the revolution, begun in 1847, and she knew it was only reasonable that he should expect her to play a role in restoring order to their restless country. She felt her cousin Franz's cold eyes resting upon her and she lifted her gaze so that she could give him a small smile. Her grandmother was right, as always. It was her inescapable duty to marry Franz Johann, so she might as well make the best of it. Her father had made the formal announcement and there would be no escape from the marriage. The Commander of the Austrian troops was already carrying news of her betrothal back to the Emperor. The wedding would be solemnised within the month. She felt the moist heat of her cousin's palm pressing against the back of her glove but, exercising supreme self-control, she managed to suffer it. She even contrived another faint smile.

The Grand Duke cleared his throat and interrupted the depressing drift of Anna's thoughts. He inclined his head in a gracious gesture towards his nephew, Prince Franz Johann.

'That was a very successful evening,' the Grand Duke said. 'Anna Teresa, you behaved with most becoming dignity, and I'm sure our Austrian guests were impressed. It is good to know that your betrothal has received official, Austrian approval. Nothing can overturn it now.'

Prince Franz Johann raised Anna's hand to his lips and pressed a damp kiss against her gloved fingers. She smiled again, although her stomach churned in instinctive rejection. How terrible it was that women were forced to endure men's loathsome embraces!

'Indeed a most successful night,' Franz Johann said. As always, his soft voice sent a faint shudder of inexplicable fear down Anna's spine. 'Nevertheless, I'm glad our Austrian guests have departed for Vienna. We do not wish them to become a permanent fixture in our midst.'

The Grand Duke nodded his agreement. 'Quite right, quite right. We don't want the Austrian soldiers here. Not at all the thing. The peasants wouldn't like it for one thing. Unreasonable people, peasants.'

Anna listened to her father with a shock of surprise. Did he always sound so eager—scrambling almost—to agree with the Prince? Why was she seeing so many things recently that she had never noticed before?

The Grand Duke cleared his throat again. 'The Duchess is exhausted,' he said. 'The Austrian officers stayed later than we expected. My wife and I are leaving soon after dawn to spend a few days at our hunting-lodge. The Duchess needs to rest and I'm sure I can leave the administration in your capable hands, Franz Johann. The crises are all in the past, are they not?'

The Prince's protuberant eyes gleamed with sudden speculation. 'I am sorry to hear that the Grand Duchess is fatigued. She is well, I trust?'

There was a pause before the Duke replied. 'Now that Anna Teresa is on the threshold of marriage, it is perhaps permissible to announce our news while she is present. The Grand Duchess . . . my wife . . . is in a delicate condition. We anticipate a happy event in October.'

'You mean my mother is to have a *baby*?' Anna blurted out. Mercifully, her comment was ignored by the other occupants of the room.

'A happy event in October?' Franz Johann repeated in a low voice. 'That is scarcely five months from now.' His face was faintly flushed as he bowed in the direction of the Grand Duchess. 'What a very *unexpected* piece of news, to be sure. But joyful, of course. I offer you both my most heartfelt felicitations.' He cleared his throat. 'You must take the greatest care of the Duchess, sir. You must not take any risks that might jeopardise the safe delivery of a son and heir.'

'Well, of course, the child may be a girl. After all, we have two daughters already,' the Duke said with as hint of apology in his voice. 'And you, Franz Johann, will remain my *chief* counsellor and advisor, whether or not the Duchess is delivered of a son.'

'But I shall no longer be your heir,' the Prince said flatly. Almost before the words had been uttered, the flush faded from his cheeks and his complexion returned to its normal state of pallor. 'I am honoured that you value my advice, sir. It has always been my privilege to serve the Duchy of Carthia, and I shall look forward to serving your son if and when that time ever comes.'

'Yes, yes. That is very good news. Just what I would expect, of course.' The Grand Duke rested his hands on the considerable expanse of his brocade-covered stomach and coughed politely. 'It is well past midnight,' he said. 'The Duchess and I will bid you farewell. There is no need to present yourself for a formal leave-taking tomorrow morning, Franz Johann. You may consider yourself dismissed, as of now.'

Prince Franz Johann acknowledged this special relaxation of the rigid rules of Court etiquette by dipping into a deep bow. He raised the Grand Duchess's hand to his lips but, in approved style, took care not to touch his mouth to her gloved finger tips. He then executed another flourishing bow in front of the Grand Duke.

'I trust Anna Teresa will be remaining in the castle here in Carlsberg,' he said. 'I should not like to be deprived of her company so soon after the announcement of our betrothal.'

The Grand Duchess spoke for the first time. 'I had hoped Anna Teresa could come with us,' she said and looked appealingly at her husband.

'Yes, quite so,' responded the Duke. 'And there's the question of a chaperon, you know, Franz. We couldn't leave her here alone with you. She's out of the schoolroom now, you know.'

Anna stifled a slightly hysterical giggle. How totally absurd everybody's conversation seemed tonight. Here she was, in a castle stuffed with two or three hundred servants, and she was only considered safe if her parents remained on the premises to act as a curb to Franz Johann's non-existent lust. She glanced surreptitiously around the room at the footmen, to see if they shared her amusement. Of course they did not. They stared unseeingly ahead, their expressions as wooden as ever. For the first time in her life, Anna Teresa wondered if any human being could possibly be as deaf and uncaring as the castle servants managed to appear.

Franz Johann gave a gesture of resignation. 'I daresay you are right, sir. But I shall miss the company of your charming daughter.'

'Well, it is good to know we are leaving everything in such capable hands. Goodnight. The Duchess and I will see you in a week's time. And Anna Teresa will seem all the prettier for a few days in the country air.'

The Grand Duke ushered his wife out of the salon, and Anna automatically sank into a deep curtsy as her parents passed. To her astonishment, the Duchess halted and pressed her pink, perfumed cheek against Anna's face. 'Goodnight, my dear,' she said.

'Goodnight, Mama.' Anna stumbled over the simple words, racking her brains to recall the last time her mother had kissed her. The lingering trace of scented powder clung beneath her nostrils, haunting in its soft fragrance.

The door shut firmly. Apart from six or seven motionless lackeys, Anna and her cousin were alone. It was, she supposed, a scandalous state of affairs and indicated something about the ruffled state of her parents' minds. She had never before been alone in the company of an unmarried man.

Franz Johann showed no sign of being overcome by impropriety in the sudden intimacy of their situation. He remained a decorous ten feet away from her. 'Did you know your mother was pregnant?' he asked, snapping his fingers in the direction of one of the lackeys.

Anna flushed with shock at his use of such an indelicate word to describe her mother's condition. Until this evening, she had never heard any subject remotely touching upon the birth of a baby discussed in mixed company. She experienced an amazing new sense of sophistication, which made her forget for a moment how very much she actually disliked her cousin.

'I asked if you knew your mother was pregnant,' Franz Johann repeated.

'No, I had no idea,' she said truthfully. Trying to sound suitably nonchalant, she added. 'It is surprising, is it not? After all, it is fifteen years since my sister Luisa was born.'

A servant had poured a large measure of brandy into Prince Franz Johann's glass and he swallowed it in a single gulp, thrusting his glass out for a second serving.

'I have to travel to Innesbad tomorrow morning,' he said, ignoring her comment. 'In fact, I ought to leave for my own estates tonight.'

'Oh, I see. Then why did you wish me to remain in Carlsberg if you are not going to be here with me?'

'What? Oh well, I had forgotten momentarily that I needed to be in Innesbad. But no matter, I shall see you when you return from the country. Perhaps it is better this way.'

'Who will take care of the affairs of state while you are away? My father left you in charge.'

Prince Franz Johann looked distinctly annoyed. 'It is not for you to question my movements, Anna Teresa. And in any case, I shall be engaged upon affairs of state during my absence. Important affairs.' Glancing up and meeting Anna's dark blue gaze, he added irritably, 'I did not inform your father because I feared it would worry him unduly.'

'I see,' Anna said again, although in fact she did not. 'You will be back soon?'

'Yes. Within a few days.' The Prince finished his third glass of brandy. At the flick of his fingers, a footman poured out another serving from the crystal decanter. Which meant that the servants were watching them after all, Anna thought irrelevantly.

'I will bid you goodnight,' she said when it was evident that her cousin had nothing further to say.

'Goodnight, Anna Teresa.' The Prince bowed low over her proffered fingers, although not as low as he had bowed over her mother's hand. His sense of protocol seemed in no danger of being overwhelmed by an upsurge of passion, Anna thought sardonically.

She shook the thought away and walked towards the gold-painted doors of the Small Salon. As she passed, a footman sprang to attention. Two more footmen pushed open the doors and held them back with white-gloved hands. Although she had never noticed it before, Anna saw that two lackeys waited for her in the Great Hall, the gold braid of their uniforms gleaming in the blazing light of the chandeliers. With great solemnity, all five footmen escorted the Princess to the foot of the marble staircase.

A serving maid, who had presumably spent most of the night huddled in the shadows of a small recess under the stairs, sprang into step between the Princess and the lackeys. She held aloft a flaming branch of candles, impervious to the hot wax that dripped on to her wrists. The entire guard-of-honour stumbled to a halt when Anna turned round suddenly to face them. She smiled sweetly.

'I can walk upstairs by myself,' she said.

Her words fell into a pool of silence. All the servants were apparently too shocked to move or speak. Princess Anna Teresa smiled at them again, then walked up the stairs to her room. For the first time in her life, she went upstairs alone.

CHAPTER
THREE

EVEN though her servants stayed up most of the night packing, Anna Teresa was late the next morning. As she had feared, the Duke and Duchess were standing in the main courtyard of the castle when she hurried downstairs an hour after dawn. She curtseyed deeply, her dove-grey travelling dress billowing into a velvet circle around her knees.

'I am sorry that I have delayed your departure, Mama and Papa.'

The Grand Duchess smiled with unexpected warmth. 'It doesn't matter, Anna Teresa. Your father and I both wanted to have you with us. It will be our last chance to spend time together as a family before your marriage next month.'

'Yes, Mama.' Anna forbore to point out that it would not only be the last chance, but also the first. She was touched by her mother's affection and she smiled with sudden happiness. 'I am so glad we are going into the country, Mama.'

'Yes, yes, we are all glad,' said the Grand Duke somewhat testily. He added, with no apparent relevance. 'Franz Johann left the castle late last night. The guards reported to me this morning.'

'He did mention to me that he had to leave for Innesbad on some matter of state, Papa. If you remember, you gave him permission to absent himself from Carlsberg.'

'I shouldn't have thought there was any need for him to go jauntering off just now,' the Grand Duke said. 'Well, do you think we might get into the carriages? We have kept the horses standing for the best part of half an hour.'

Three carriages awaited the pleasure of their party. One old-fashioned coach was already piled high with a great deal of crested luggage. The two other carriages stood empty, flanked by military outriders.

'You shall travel with us, so that we may converse,' said the Grand Duchess to her daughter.

The royal travelling phaeton was less than three years old, imported from the English coach-building firm patronised by Queen Victoria. Anna had never travelled in it before, since the rebellious state of the countryside over the last two years had prevented pleasure trips outside the safe boundaries of the castle walls. Even trips into the capital city of Carlsberg had been few and far between since she left the schoolroom. She sank back against the soft, padded leather of the seat, feeling the excellent springs that cushioned the bumping motion of the iron wheels as they rolled over the cobbled castle driveway.

'What a lovely day it promises to be!' she exclaimed, peering out of the window at the sun rising in the clear sky of a late spring day.

The Grand Duke smiled indulgently, ignoring her breach of etiquette in speaking before he had started a conversation. 'I see that your mother was correct, my dear. You have been feeling unsettled these past few months, have you not?'

Anna looked at her mother in surprise. She had not thought her restlessness had been so obvious.

'We have all been confined too much to the castle,' she said at last. 'And I miss my governess. She was my only true . . . I mean to say, she was a good friend to me.'

'Ah yes,' said the Duke. 'Miss . . . er . . . The English spinster. She was very attached to you.'

'Miss Frobisher,' Anna said, conscious of a faint spurt of resentment. Her governess had lived in the castle for fifteen years. Was it too much to hope that the Grand Duke should remember her name? 'She was a very good teacher, Papa. She told such wonderful stories about England.'

'We would have found you a new companion, Anna Teresa, if the revolution had not occupied all your father's attention over the past eighteen months.' The Duchess touched her daughter lightly on the arm.

'No need for another fussy female now,' the Grand Duke remarked. 'You will have a husband and lifelong companion this time next month.' He gave a sigh of satisfaction. 'It is a relief to know that the dangers of the revolution are past. It's too long since I have been able to indulge in the excitement of the hunt.'

'Yes, Papa.' Anna did not want to think about Franz Johann and the fact that he would soon be her 'lifelong companion', so she watched the tree-covered hills pass by the carriage window. It was a peaceful scene, the sunlight touching the cottage roofs with golden warmth, the tall pines thrusting against the blue of the sky in a powerful dark green barrier. She heard the tinkle of goat bells and the occasional lowing of a cow, seeking pasture, but for the most part she was conscious of the utter quiet of the countryside.

'Where are all the people?' she aked suddenly, struck by the deserted nature of the villages they were passing. Their carriages bore the royal coat-of-arms prominently displayed, and, in days gone by, groups of waving children had always greeted the passage of the Grand Duke's coach.

Her mother's face flushed. 'The peasants stay inside their cottages these days,' she said.

The Grand Duke looked at his daughter with a hint of irritation. 'You have been protected from reality within the walls of the castle, Anna Teresa. But you are old enough to be aware of the fact that a few hot-headed rabble-rousers have managed, during the last two years, to destroy the generations of peace my people previously enjoyed. The university my grandfather was generous enough to establish even had the audacity to elect Carthian representatives to attend that Parliament of Revolutionaries in Frankfurt. As if my subjects have any right to suggest how I should govern my duchy! And as for Stefan . . . ! That supposed brother of Franz Johann . . .' The Duke stopped hastily as his wife pressed her fingers against his arm.

'Well, enough said,' the Duke continued. 'No need to sully your ears with information about that dreadful fellow. You will never meet him, thank God. Certainly, he and the peasants are fools if they think their lot in life would be improved by changing the yoke of Austrian control for domination by Prussia and its government of military autocrats. They would find out just what taxation and military service really can mean if Prussia ever controlled the German empire.' He shook his shoulders, as if to remove the annoyance of an unwelcome train of thought. 'I don't even want to think about the idiocy of a unified Germany. There is no such nation except in the minds of a few misguided and impractical dreamers.'

'I don't altogether understand what the revolution was about, Papa.'

'There is no need for you to worry about understanding difficult political matters, Anna Teresa,' the Duchess reproved her gently. 'Once you are married, your cousin Franz will help you to understand whatever few facts you need to know. You do not have to trouble yourself with comprehending every detail of the Austrian and German political scene. Your cousin will explain to you exactly what you have to think about everything.'

'Yes, of course, Mama.' Anna Teresa nodded submissively, but the morning's sunshine seemed suddenly to have lost some of its brilliance. What if she didn't agree with her cousin's opinions? What if she found his ideas unacceptable? Impossible. She thrust the errant thoughts aside. It was her duty to agree with Prince Franz Johann, and she had spent a lifetime training to do her duty.

Their phaeton, surrounded by outriders, reached the edges of the dense woods where the hunting-lodge was located while Anna was lost in her unsatisfactory thoughts. She shivered slightly as the coach passed out of the warm sunlight into the shadowed depths of the forest. It was nearly four years since she had made this journey and the trees seemed thicker than she remembered, the road narrower and more overgrown.

The Duke and Duchess shared none of her vague apprehension. They did not bother to look out at the gloomy scenery, but chatted together cosily, the Duke stroking his wife's wrist tenderly with his thumb. The Grand Duchess looked up and happened to catch Anna's eyes. Her mouth softened into a sweet smile.

'Oh my God! My dear heart!' The Duke's voice rose in a shouted cry of outrage as the carriage plunged to a screeching halt. The Duchess crumpled into her husband's arms, blood spurting from the gaping grenade wound blasted in her side. Even as the Duke cradled his wife's body, he leaned across the carriage and thrust Anna face down on the floor. He stuck his foot on her neck when she attempted to get up.

Anna heard another explosion inside the carriage and felt the weight of her father's body fall across her back and legs. Her mother, still clasped in the Duke's arms, slipped out of the carriage seat and her embroidered cream crinoline—spattered now with scarlet—fell in a whispering sigh over Anna's head.

Fresh rifle shots exploded all around them and above the explosion of the bullets, Anna could hear the sickening shriek of wounded horses and the dull thud of bodies falling to the ground. A woman was screaming with a constant, high-pitched monotony that reverberated inside Anna's head. The screaming finally stopped with an abrupt, brutal silence which was worse than the noise that had gone before.

Anna lay unmoving on the floor of the carriage, not consciously hiding herself, but too petrified with shock to be capable of movement. She felt the door of the phaeton jerk open, the fine springs of the new carriage causing it to sway with a violent rocking motion. She smelled the sweat of the murderer's overheated body, but she experienced no sensation of personal danger because her mind was frozen into blankness. She sensed, rather than heard, the cursory examination the man gave to the blood-spattered carriage interior. Her mind was too stunned to assimilate the guttural comment that the assassin called out to his unseen colleagues.

The carriage door slammed shut. She heard the sounds of horses galloping away. The hoofbeats faded into the distance and silence descended once more upon the forest. From far away, she heard the bell-like call of the cuckoo. She still did not attempt to move, although the weight of her father's body was agonising on her spine, and the skirts of her mother's crinoline were suffocating her.

She let the thick lace of her mother's petticoats drift against her nose, while she prayed for oblivion to consume her and blot out the nightmare images of the past few minutes. But she remained obstinately, painfully, alive.

She had no idea how long she lay on the padded floor of the coach, motionless except for the choked whisper of her breath and the faint, jerky thud of her heartbeat. At last she heard the distant barking of a dog and the sound galvanised her into action as nothing else had done. The fright which had not so far touched her, suddenly gripped her tight. She had no idea whether the dogs represented a real threat or a hope of rescue, but she could taste the fear in her mouth as she listened to their harsh barking. Her throat closed up, her stomach churned and her legs trembled so that she wondered if she would be able to stand.

She gripped the edge of the seat and pulled herself out from beneath her parents' dead bodies. Her mother's face still smiled in death. Her father no longer had a face. She turned away quickly, but not quickly enough, and she retched helplessly, unable to control the sickness welling up inside her.

The barking of the dogs was getting ominously close, and her volatile emotions coalesced into panic. She thrust open the coach door, scarcely noticing that her father's body slipped on to the carriage steps as the door burst open. She clambered over him, down on to the stony road, averting her eyes from the nauseating evidence of carnage that lay all around her. She recognised the bronze velvet skirt of her lady-in-waiting, who lay with her face buried in a pile of soft earth.

Anna's body was seized with a fresh fit of shivering and she stood stock-still, incapable of thought or movement. The sound of a man's voice, shouted over the barking of the dogs, jerked her into action. Her mind was still incapable of rational thought, but her body forced her to try to escape from the clutches of the men who had slaughtered her parents and all the court attendants. There was not even an animal left alive.

She did not know how far she was from the royal hunting-lodge. She only knew that the dark shadows of the forest beckoned her with a welcome promise of concealment, invisibility, *sanctuary*. She ran, panting and sobbing, in the direction of the thickest foliage she could see. She ignored the brambles that tore at her skirts and stained her face, so that berry juice mingled with blood stains in a gruesome pattern. She was heedless of the low branches that ripped her jacket and tore the jewelled pins from her hair.

She only stopped running when she was too

exhausted to go any further. She collapsed in a huddle on the ground, her body shuddering as she drew great gulps of air into her burning lungs. She was afraid to shut her eyes, so she stared at the ants that crawled over her hands, concentrating her mind on their endless circling, so that she would not have to think about anything else.

'Are you a witch?'

For a moment, Anna's heart stopped beating, before starting to pound harder than ever against the wall of her chest. She turned round sharply, crouching like an animal at bay. A thin, grubby child, her skin burned dark brown by exposure to the open air, stood a few feet from Anna. In her hand she clenched an iron crucifix, which she held prominently in front of her.

Anna licked her parched lips. 'I'm not a witch,' she tried to say. She knew that the croak she made was incomprehensible and she swallowed hard. 'I'm not a witch,' she said again.

'You're mad then,' the child said with a philosophical acceptance of the inevitable. Anna noticed that she still kept the iron crucifix held protectively high in front of her.

'Not that either.' Anna's gasp of laughter rose higher and ended in a harsh sob. She clamped her lips together to cut off the sound. She could taste blood and grit inside her mouth.

'If you aren't a witch and you aren't mad, why are you lying in the witches' circle?'

'I didn't know it was the witches' circle.' Anna managed to sit up straighter, and tried to push the hair out of her eyes.

'Everybody knows this is where the witches come to dance at night,' the child said scornfully. 'It's

dangerous. Besides, all these woods belong to the
Grand Duke.'

'Then why are *you* here?'

The child examined Anna thoughtfully. 'Are you
sure you aren't mad?' she asked.

'Quite sure,' Anna said, then wondered fleet-
ingly if she spoke the truth.

'My grandma and I have to eat, so I come to pick
marsh marigolds. You know, cowslips. My gran
makes marigold wine and sells it. The best flowers
are here, because the other girls are too scared to
come so far on to the Duke's land. And they're
afraid of the witches' circle. But I brought my iron
cross, and I'm not frightened.'

Anna frowned, wondering if she had correctly
understood the child's dialect. 'But wine is made
from grapes, not from . . . cowslips . . .' she said.

The girl shrugged, not bothering to reply, but she
allowed the crucifix to fall back against her thin
neck. No witch, she seemed to have concluded,
could waste time talking so much nonsense. She set
about picking flowers without paying any further
attention to Anna.

They continued to sit in silence for some minutes. 'Are you going to sit there all day?' the girl
asked finally. 'If you've got nothing else to do, you
could pick some flowers.'

Anna glanced surreptitiously at the girl's basket.
Although she had no intention of increasing the
child's suspicions by admitting her ignorance, she
had no idea what marsh marigolds looked like.
They were a fragile, pale yellow flower, she saw,
with a protuberant golden heart. She picked a
handful and handed them to the child.

'There,' she said. 'Do you have enough now?'

The girl looked at her, scorn and amusement mingled in her expression. 'I know what it is,' she said. 'You're not exactly mad. You're simple. Feeble-minded. Why aren't they taking care of you in your own village? You shouldn't be wandering around on your own.'

Anna breathed in sharply, cutting off the angry retort that formed on her lips. The child, after all, didn't know she was talking to the daughter of the Grand Duke of Carthia. 'I'm lost,' she said finally. 'Could you help me find my way out of the forest?'

'If you can tell me which way you want to go,' replied the girl.

The sound sense of this remark was less than welcome, since Anna had no idea where she ought to go, or what she ought to do next. How long would it be before it was safe to make her true identity known? This child represented no threat, but what about the child's father and brothers? Perhaps they were revolutionaries. Who had planned the massacre? Whom could she trust when her world had turned itself upside down?

She remembered Franz Johann with a sudden burst of relief. Her cousin's estates were somewhere in this area, and he would take care of her until the assassins were found and punished. Prince Franz Johann was her fiancé as well as her cousin, and he was her natural protector.

'Do you know the town of Innesbad?' she asked the girl. 'It's at the centre of the estates of Prince Franz Johann, heir to the Duke of Carthia.' As she spoke, she was struck by the realisation that her cousin was no longer heir to the dukedom. He *was* the new Grand Duke of Carthia. Poor Mama, she thought, I wonder if your baby would have been a boy.

'You want to go *back* to Innesbad?' the girl asked. She looked at Anna with a world of cynical knowledge in her young face. 'I've heard tell 'tis a good place to run away from.'

Anna failed to conceal her shock. 'You surely cannot mean to suggest that His Highness the Prince . . . that Prince Franz Johann is not a good ruler . . .' She could scarcely manage to complete her sentence.

The child's face closed into a mask of blankness. 'I didn't mean anything,' she said. 'I didn't say anything, either. I'll set you on the road to Innesbad if that's what you want. It isn't above twelve miles from here. You can walk it before nightfall, easy.'

'Twelve miles! I can't walk that far! Couldn't somebody lend me a horse?'

'Yes, sure we can. And a carriage with velvet seats and silk window curtains, and all. I'll take your ladyship to my own private stables when I've finished picking these flowers for my gran.'

'Thank you,' Anna said, marvelling to herself at the strange economic arrangements peasants obviously made. She would have thought any girl would buy herself some shoes before setting up a stable of carriages and horses. But then, her grandmother had frequently reminded her that the ways of peasants were unfathomable. It was only Miss Frobisher who had insisted that, deep down, human beings were remarkably similar.

She picked some more flowers for the child while she thought. She would have to pay for the hire of the carriage. She touched her fingers to her throat.

She was, thank Heaven, wearing a strand of pearls as well as her heavy diamond betrothal ring. She had no idea how much it cost to rent a vehicle, but she thought that a string of pearls ought to cover the charge. She hoped so, anyway.

The child's basket was soon full. 'Come on,' she said. 'I'll take you to the stream so you can have a drink. You look hot.'

It seemed to Anna that they had pushed their way through miles of brambles before they arrived at the promised stream. She splashed water over her face and washed her hands, lifting up the ripped and stained edge of her velvet gown to dry her hands on the lace trimmings of her petticoats. No wonder the child had accused her of being a witch, she thought wryly. She certainly looked a great deal more like a witch than a princess. She hoped her cousin Franz would not be shocked by her filthy, blood-stained appearance. Even he, stickler for propriety that he was, could not expect her to survive an assassination attempt totally unscathed.

The brief thought of the massacre was too painful to allow back into her mind and she spoke quickly, before the brutal images could re-imprint themselves on her consciousness.

'Is it far from here to your home?'

'No. Gran lives close to the edge of the forest. But your road isn't the same as mine. Our paths separate up there.' The girl pointed through the thinning trees of the forest. 'You follow the right-hand track all the way into Innesbad. I have to take the other path to my gran's cottage.'

Anna's blue eyes darkened in bewilderment. 'But where are the horses and carriages?' she asked uncertainly. 'You said you kept a stable. I can pay you for their hire, you know. You don't have to worry.'

'You *are* daft,' the child said. 'You're stark mad. I should have left you in the witches' circle. Where do you think I'd find money for a fancy carriage? And don't you know the Grand Duke requisitioned every horse in the country more than a year ago? I should have thought everybody knew that, even mad people from Innesbad.'

'The Duke requisitioned every horse?' Anna said faintly. 'You must be mistaken.' The horrendous events of the day caught up with her at last, and to her dismay she felt the tears start to stream down her cheeks. 'I can't walk twelve miles,' she said. 'I'm so tired.'

The girl watched Anna's tears in silence, as if struggling with some inner conflict. Finally, she thrust a cotton-wrapped packet into Anna's hands. 'Here, take this. And you'd better be moving if you want to reach Innesbad before nightfall. It doesn't do to get caught in these woods after dark. Nor on the streets of Innesbad, neither.' Without waiting for Anna to speak, she darted off down the path, disappearing into the tangle of thicket.

Anna stuffed her fist into her mouth and swallowed the beginning of another hysterical sob. 'Wait!' she called out to the child. 'Wait! Please! I'm a princess . . . I'm the Princess Anna Teresa . . .'

The sound of her voice echoed back from the empty woods. She was alone again, and the dark pines and luxuriant undergrowth suddenly looked more like a prison than a sanctuary. Anna fought back the panic and stared at the long, deserted path twisting to the right of her. She could only hope that the child was correct and that it did indeed lead to Franz Johann's castle. With a weary shrug of resignation, she set her feet on to the stony track.

She walked for hours, or at least it seemed like hours, her body passing from individual areas of pain into one, single, solidified mass of misery. It was some time before she realised that the gnawing ache in her middle was probably caused by hunger. She remembered the packet the child had given her and she untied the knots of cotton with eager, fumbling fingers. Two small slices of grey rye bread and a lump of fat sausage nestled in the ragged folds.

Princess Anna Teresa of Carthia looked dubiously at the stale food. Then, with a small sigh, she sank on to a hummock of grass and hungrily ate her dinner.

CHAPTER
FOUR

THE sun had set when Anna finally left the woods. A milestone, stuck at the side of the road, warned her that it was still three miles to the town of Innesbad but she was too exhausted to worry. She placed one leaden foot in front of the other and plodded on, her head down because it required too much effort to hold it up.

At last the walls of the old city loomed ahead of her in the darkness. She peered thankfully at the crenellated stone turrets of the wall. They were black against the darkness of the night sky. There was no guard posted at the gateway to the city, and she passed quickly under the stone arch bearing the Count of Innesbad's coat-of-arms.

She was sure it couldn't be very late, although her watch had been lost hours ago. But the streets of the town were deserted, the houses shuttered and quiet. She hurried along the empty pavements, her worn kid slippers making little noise on the cobblestones. The unnatural silence unnerved her, although she tried not to admit this was so. She followed the signs that pointed to the Market Place. Surely there—in the centre of the town—she would find somebody to escort her to the Prince's castle. Unless he had been murdered too. She shuddered at the terrifying thought, pushing it to the back of her mind before panic could overwhelm her.

'Halt! Show me your pass!'

She whirled around and saw three soldiers, wearing the familiar uniforms of her cousin's bodyguard. She ran towards them with the last of her strength.

'Thank God I have found you!' she exclaimed. 'Take me to Prince Franz Johann immediately.'

One of the soldiers grasped her roughly by the arm and she froze at his touch. 'How *dare* you!' she said icily. 'Remove your hand from my person *at once*! Do you not recognise who I am?'

The soldier merely held her tighter. 'Where are your papers?' he asked. From the stripes on his sleeve, she realised he was a sergeant.

'I am the Princess Anna Teresa,' she said haughtily. 'I am ordering you to take me to Prince Franz Johann.'

The youngest of the three soldiers snapped instantly to rigid attention, but the sergeant looked at him scornfully.

'At ease, soldier. The Princess Anna Teresa is resting in her coffin at Carlsberg Cathedral. You know her whole family was murdered by revolutionary scum this morning. What are you saluting this lying bitch for? She's probably one of the murderers' whores come back to gloat over her crime.'

The sergeant shook Anna roughly by the shoulder. 'Where are your papers, woman? Don't you know that the new Grand Duke has imposed a curfew?'

'The Princess Anna Teresa is in her coffin . . .' Anna repeated dazedly. 'But she can't be. I'm here!' She covered her face with her hands and began to cry, her body heaving with inelegant, shuddering sobs. 'What have they done? Who have they put with Mama and Papa? Why have they said I am dead?'

'Because you are, of course,' said the sergeant roughly. 'That is, I mean to say, the Princess Anna Teresa is dead. Come along now. Give over acting this way, or I'll lock you up for the night. Get out of Innesbad, or it'll be the castle dungeons for you, my girl.'

'There has been a terrible mistake,' Anna said. Drawing herself up as straight as she could, she tried to gather the shattered remnants of her dignity. 'I am the Princess Anna Teresa. I survived the assassination attempt this morning, and I *demand* that you take me to my cousin, the new Grand Duke of Carthia.'

Just for a moment, there was an uneasy silence among the soldiers. The sergeant recovered his voice first. 'I'll take you to the Duke on a charge of treason, if you're not careful,' he blustered.

The youngest soldier snapped to attention. 'Permission to speak, sergeant.'

'Granted.'

'What if there has been a mistake? What if she *is* the Princess?' He lowered his voice and said almost in a whisper. 'She's wearing jewels, sergeant. And her clothes are made of silk and velvet. You can see if you look under the dirt.'

'There's a name for women who wear fancy clothes like her,' the sergeant said. His expression, however, was nowhere near as confident as his voice.

'Search her,' he said at last. 'If she has no weapons, I'll take her to the Captain of the Castle Guard. Let him decide what to do with her.'

One of the soldiers held Anna still, while the other ran his hands all over her body. He was sweating by the time he had finished the task.

'It's my job, you understand. I have to do it,' he said. 'I saw the Princess in the cathedral this morning, laid out, deader than dead. You understand why I have to search you, don't you?'

Anna could not bring herself to meet the soldier's eyes. She felt defiled by the touch of his hands on her body. 'Take me to the Grand Duke,' she said finally. 'You have discovered for yourself that I am carrying no weapons.'

The soldiers marched one on either side of her, and the sergeant brought up the rear. They were an oddly silent group as they paraded through the town and up the winding path that led to the castle, perched on a hill brooding over the city.

Anna had thought she was tired before. During the climb she discovered that she had scarcely begun to plumb the depths of exhaustion that the human body could endure while still continuing to function. She was conscious, but only just when they entered the castle barracks. Her eyes were blurred by cold sweat and her lungs were burning when the sergeant called a halt to their brisk march and stood at attention in front of the Captain of the Guard.

'Well, well, what have we here?' asked the Captain, placing his hand casually beneath Anna's chin and jerking her face up for a quick inspection.

'If you please, sir, she says she is the Princess Anna Teresa. She wishes to see His Serene Highness, Prince Franz Johann.' The sergeant corrected himself hastily. 'That is to say, she wishes to see His

Serene Highness, the Grand Duke Franz Johann of
Carthia.'

'Throw her in one of the castle dungeons,' the
Captain said curtly. 'Tell the prison governor she is
being held on a charge of high treason. Give her ten
lashes before she's handed over to the jailer. It's
time these peasants were taught to keep their mad-
women under control.'

'How dare you order a whipping!' Anna exclaimed, scarcely registering that she was the
woman destined to be on the end of the lash. 'It is
illegal to whip a prisoner before the judge has
pronounced a verdict of guilty. Torture has been
outlawed in Carthia for 136 years. I shall see to it
that my cousin hears of the false justice his guards
are perpetrating in his name.'

The Captain did not even bother to look around.
'Thirty lashes,' he said.

'Yes, sir.' The sergeant did not move and the
Captain turned to him irritably. 'Why are you
waiting, sergeant?'

The soldier stirred uneasily, shifting from one
foot to the other. 'With the Captain's permission to
speak, sir, the prisoner is wearing jewels on her
neck and on her hands. The prisoner is also wearing
very costly clothing, sir, if you look under all the
dirt. And the prisoner asked for an audience with
His Highness, the Grand Duke Franz Johann, sir.
She is carrying no weapons, so why should she ask
to see the Grand Duke, unless . . . unless . . .'

'Are you suggesting, sergeant, that we have here
the Princess Anna Teresa? You think, possibly,
that she has arisen from the dead and come to pay a
personal call on you?'

'No, sir.'

'Then just what are you suggesting, sergeant?'

'Perhaps she is the Princess's lady-in-waiting, sir. Perhaps she was a witness to the assassination and is now unhinged. You know, sir. Mad. But I don't think we ought to throw a court official into the dungeons, sir. And she does talk like a member of the court, not like a peasant, sir.'

The Captain looked at Anna with a sudden spark of interest. 'Lady-in-waiting . . .' he murmured. His eyes stared absently into the distance as if considering a new and intriguing idea. He turned back to Anna with unexpected sharpness. 'Describe the State Apartments at the Grand Duke's castle to me.' Her gaze flickered over him scornfully. 'It is not my custom to describe anything to a captain of my cousin's bodyguard.'

The sergeant waited for an explosion of wrath from the Captain, but it never came. The Captain merely examined Anna more closely, his eyes narrowing as he scrutinised the betrothal ring on her slim finger.

'You are dismissed,' he said to the soldiers suddenly. 'And you had better forget that you ever found this prisoner, is that clear?'

'Yes, sir!' The sergeant saluted smartly and the three soldiers retreated from the barracks as swiftly as they could.

When they were alone, the Captain conducted Anna into a small private room adjoining his guard-post. 'I shall find hot water, towels and brushes for you, Your . . . er . . . Highness. You will wish to tidy yourself before I escort you into the presence of the Grand Duke.'

'Oh, at last somebody is listening to me!' Anna sank on to the hard wooden chair, forcing back her unfounded mistrust of the Captain. 'Thank Heaven!' she said. 'I shall see that my cousin rewards you suitably.'

The Captain's eyes narrowed again, and then he smiled. 'Indeed, I anticipate a reward,' he said softly. 'Now, rest for a few minutes, Your Highness, while I make arrangements for your refreshment. I regret that there will be no maidservant to assist you.'

'It doesn't matter. I shall manage.'

The Captain bowed and retreated very correctly from the room, never once turning his back upon the Princess.

Anna Teresa sighed with relief when the door closed behind him. She didn't like the Captain and she was glad to be alone. There was a mirror in the corner of the room, and she walked slowly towards it. She stopped, several feet away, almost afraid to get any closer. A cold-eyed, wild-haired girl stared out of the shadowed depths of the glass. The lace of her bodice was ripped away from the velvet seams of her dress, revealing slashes of white skin. Her hair, unrestrained by a single pin, cascaded over her shoulders in a tangled mass of dusty chestnut curls. But it was her expression that frightened Anna most. The familiar round contours of her cheeks had vanished. The delicate fullness of her lips had tightened into a wary line, hard and suspicious in its form. She looked years older, Anna realised with a profound sense of shock. Only a year or two older physically, but a hundred years older in the new knowledge that lingered at the back of her eyes.

There was a quiet knock at the door. 'Enter!' she said.

The Captain came in bearing a steaming metal jug and a selection of towels. He placed the jug next to a china washbowl and indicated to Anna that he had provided her with brushes and combs as well as hot water.

'Thank you,' she said, trying to inject some friendliness into her voice.

The Captain bowed. 'I shall be waiting in the outer office. When Your Highness is ready to meet the Grand Duke, I shall escort you personally.'

She inclined her head in acknowledgement, waiting until the Captain had once again bowed himself out of the room before she turned to the washing stand.

She quickly discovered that cleaning herself in a small bowl of hot water was not quite the same thing as having a personal maid assist her in a perfumed bath, but she also made the discovery that standards of comfort were relative. In comparison to the day she had just endured, and in comparison to washing in the cold water of a woodland spring, the Captain's pottery washbowl seemed positively luxurious. She tried to brush the dust out of her hair, but there was so much caked dirt embedded in the long strands that it was almost impossible. She had no pins, so she tore a strip from her petticoat and tied the dirty curls back in a thick braid. It was embarrassing to contemplate meeting her cousin Franz with her hair in disarray and a bruise darkening her cheek, but the events of the day had left her with an indifference to convention she would not have believed possible only twenty-four hours previously. She unconsciously squared her shoulders before walking into the Captain's office.

'I am ready.'

He sprang to his feet. 'I shall escort you to the Grand Duke immediately, Your Highness.' She couldn't identify the emotion she heard in his voice, hiding behind the polite words.

The long, stone-walled corridors were chilly, but Anna scarcely noticed the gloomy surroundings. Her grandmother would be amused, she thought wryly. Neither of them, in their wildest fancies, had ever imagined Anna could feel such happiness at the mere prospect of seeing Franz Johann. Her heart was actually beating fast with relief and excitement. How delighted her cousin would be to discover she had not been killed in the massacre! How extraordinary it was that he had made the mistake of identifying another woman as the Princess Anna Teresa! It must be the poor lady-in-waiting who was lying in state at the cathedral, Anna reflected. The poor woman had had auburn hair, not quite the same colour . . . She suddenly realised what a dreadful shock her cousin was about to receive, and she spoke quickly to the Captain.

'Have you sent word to the Grand Duke that I am alive? It will be too great a surprise for him otherwise.'

'The Grand Duke knows of your arrival in the castle,' replied the Captain.

They started to climb a steep staircase that led, Anna assumed, to the State Apartments. They emerged in a low, narrow corridor, whose walls were hung with green silk, flocked in velvet. The corridor was exceptionally quiet, and Anna realised that during their entire journey from the barracks they had not encountered a single servant.

With the instinctive suspicion that was so new to her, she spun round to confront the Captain.

'Where are you taking me? This cannot be the way to the official reception rooms.'

'Of course not, Your Highness. You have forgotten how late it is. The Grand Duke is waiting for you in his private suite. He is, in any case, in deep mourning for his massacred relatives. He has been in his private rooms ever since attending the cathedral to pray for the souls of his aunt and uncle, and for his cousin. Although we now know that his prayers for the Princess Anna Teresa were not needed . . .' The Captain smiled smoothly as he finished speaking.

'Why are there no footmen in the halls?'

The Captain only hesitated for a second or two before answering. 'I conducted Your Highness along a system of private corridors. I felt sure you would wish to avoid the public gaze as much as possible.'

He knocked discreetly at a felt-covered door as he finished speaking.

'Who is it?' a man said, and Anna recognised her cousin's voice.

'It is Captain von Drucker, Your Highness.'

'Enter.'

The Captain opened the door, and Anna preceded him into the room. Her cousin sat in front of a blazing fire and she was so glad to see him that her eyes were blind to every other detail of the room. 'Franz! Thank God!' she exclaimed. She rushed across the room, feeling the tears forming in her eyes now that it was safe to cry. 'Oh Franz! You can't imagine what it has been like . . . How terrible it was in the carriage when they shot my parents. First Mama, then Papa . . . Oh God! I cannot bear to think of it . . .'

'Who is this madwoman?' Franz Johann asked coldly.

In her agitation, she had sunk on to a footstool close to her cousin's chair. Franz Johann rose to his feet and, with a gesture of profound revulsion, unclasped her fingers from his arm, where they had curled convulsively.

For a moment, Anna's heart froze with fear, then she laughed very shakily. 'Franz, I realise I have changed a great deal in the past twelve hours, but look at me closely. It is I, Anna Teresa, your cousin and your promised wife.'

For a split second his eyes locked with her own and in that minute she knew—incontrovertibly and beyond the possibility of doubt—that her cousin Franz had recognised her. He turned away quickly, veiling his eyes. He looked over her shoulder and spoke in glacial tones to the Captain.

'Why did you bring this woman to me? Why did you disturb my period of bitter mourning by introducing a madwoman into my presence?'

The Captain snapped the heels of his boots together and stood even more rigidly at attention, before bending his head in a gesture of apology. But his voice, Anna realised, was not apologetic at all. It was faintly threatening.

'I thought it possible, Your Highness, that the madwoman might be lady-in-waiting to the late Princess Anna Teresa, your . . . beloved . . . fiancé. I wondered if she might have lost the balance of her mind when she witnessed the dreadful massacre this morning. I thought you would certainly recognise the Princess's lady-in-waiting . . .'

Anna forced herself out of the daze that seemed to bind her to the chair.

'Franz—what does he mean? What is he implying? Why will you not admit to him that I am Anna Teresa? What have I done to displease you so dreadfully?'

Franz Johann's cold gaze brushed over her tears. 'Be silent, woman, or you will find yourself unable to speak.' He turned back to the Captain. 'You see for yourself that she is raving. Why should you think she is lady-in-waiting to the Princess?'

'You will remember that I rode this morning with Your Highness to the actual site of the massacre. You will remember that we found the body of the former Grand Duke's equerry. We found the body of the Grand Duchess's lady-in-waiting. But we did not find the body of the Princess's lady-in-waiting. If you remember, Your Highness, you personally ordered my troops to search the woods near the scene of the . . . dreadful . . . crime. Looking back on the terrible events of this morning, it does now seem to me that Your Highness was acting as though you believed somebody had escaped the assassin's fire. You were, I now realise, expecting to find another body. The lady-in-waiting, perhaps . . . or at any rate, somebody.'

'You are an enterprising young man, Captain von Drucker.'

The Captain acknowledged the compliment with another click of his heels. 'I brought this prisoner to you because she presents something of a problem for Your Highness. Her clothes and manner, you see, not to mention her jewels, are those of a noblewoman. And have you observed the crested betrothal ring that she wears?' Captain von Drucker looked at the Grand Duke with eyes that gleamed in open challenge. 'I was afraid that the prisoner might convince some gullible troublemakers that her story is true, that she is indeed the Princess Anna Teresa. In the unsettled state of our beloved duchy, I knew you could not afford to have rumours flying about the countryside . . . And so, Your Highness, I brought the poor madwoman to you.'

'How wonderfully quick-witted of you, Captain von Drucker. We must see that you are suitably rewarded for your marvellous powers of reasoning.'

'Thank you, Your Highness.'

'I trust your quick-thinking extended to ensuring that nobody else knows of the arrival of this prisoner in my castle?'

'Naturally, I took every precaution, Your Highness. There is the problem of the soldiers who found her wandering in the town, of course.'

Franz Johann looked up swiftly. 'Find them,' he ordered softly.

'Yes, Your Highness. As it happens, we need three more recruits to fill our quota for the Austrian Imperial Army. Those three would be perfect candidates.'

Franz Johann smiled. 'I can see that we shall work well together, Captain von Drucker.'

Anna looked from the Captain to her cousin and back again, her heart leaden with despair. She forced herself to face her cousin, although she knew already that it was useless to plead her cause.

'Franz Johann, why are you doing this to me?' she asked. 'Please tell me how I have offended you.'

'I have already ordered you to remain silent.'
Almost without pause, he added. 'You are dismissed, Colonel von Drucker.'

The new colonel smiled his gratification. 'You will not regret my promotion, Your Highness.'

'I am sure I shall not,' agreed Franz Johann. 'But Colonel, I beg to point out to you that too accurate a memory might prove disastrous to your continued success in the military.'

'I am notorious for my forgetfulness, Your Highness.'

'What a fortunate situation for both of us. Go back the way you came, dear fellow. There is no need to advertise this evening's affairs.'

Anna watched Colonel von Drucker retreat through the same door that had admitted them to the Duke's rooms. It was, she observed, cleverly hidden in the silk panelling of the walls.

'Intriguing, is it not? remarked Franz Johann, noticing the direction of her gaze. 'My father and grandfather used those corridors for the discreet importation of their lady loves. I find it has other, more practical uses.'

'You should take care,' Anna said bitterly. 'One of these days an assassin will find his way up those hidden stairs.'

'But not, I think, while Colonel von Drucker and his men guard the only entrance to the corridors,' Franz Johann said lightly. 'An admirable man our Colonel von Drucker, but perhaps just a touch too ambitious for his own good.' With no perceptible change in his manner, he added, 'Give me the betrothal ring you are wearing. You should not have stolen it from Princess Anna Teresa.'

She took off the ring, looking at him sadly.

'Don't lie when we're alone, Franz. You know who I am.'

He took the ring and dropped it into his pocket. He did not look at Anna.

'Franz, what has happened? Three days ago you stood in my father's presence and told him you would cherish me all the days of our lives. Is this how you keep that promise?'

'Three days ago your father was Grand Duke of Carthia and he had neglected to tell me his wife was expecting a child. Two days ago, it seemed quite possible that I would be replaced as heir by a baby who would undoubtedly have been trained to be as weak-willed as its father. Today, I am the Grand Duke of Carthia. A lot may happen in three days.'

'What has all this to do with your promise to me?' Anna asked in a low voice.

'I told Anna Teresa to remain in the castle. She chose to accompany her mother and father, and her fate was sealed. If she had done as I asked, she would have been quite safe. I have no particular quarrel with Anna Teresa. Her sister the Princess Luisa, is unharmed. The Dowager Grand Duchess is unharmed. Perhaps, when my grief over Princess Anna Teresa has faded, I shall marry Luisa. *She* is young enough to be subjected to my will.'

The full implications of what her cousin was saying slowly penetrated Anna Teresa's jumbled thoughts. Her face went grey.

'You are telling me . . . You are saying, are you not, that you ordered the assassination of my parents? And all because my mother was expecting a baby, who might not even have been a boy?'

'Tut, tut. You are madder than I feared. It is

well-known that the massacre was organised by revolutionaries. At this very moment I am preparing to execute the villains who perpetrated the foul deed.'

'More innocent victims?'

'Revolutionaries can never be innocent, my dear. If they took no part in this crime, they surely took part in some other. Why don't you help yourself to some wine and cake from the table over there? But pray do not interrupt me with any further useless pleas and idle chatter. I need silence in which to think.'

Anna Teresa wanted very much to behave with dignity, but her knees would no longer support her and she sank into a huddle on the floor. 'Wh-what are you going to do with me?' she asked. 'How are you going to kill me?'

Franz Johann eased himself into the comfort of the fireside armchair. 'That is an interesting question,' he said. 'Nowadays it can be so damnably difficult to get rid of a body. So many people whom one has to bribe to remain silent, and those cursed revolutionaries, for ever ranting about democracy and honest government. My ancestors in the Middle Ages were more fortunate. They could toss a dead body out of the castle windows and wait for the wolves to eliminate the remains.' He placed his fingertips together and examined them meditatively. 'I see the beginnings of an amusing idea. It would solve two tiresome problems at one stroke. But I need to think in silence. Eat, madwoman. And remain quiet.'

It seemed foolish to stoke her body with food when her life was about to be taken from her. On the other hand, there didn't seem to be much point in suffering all the additional discomfort of a gnawing hunger. Anna seated herself on the satin-covered chair beside the table Franz Johann had indicated, and poured herself a large tumbler of wine. There were several different varieties of cake and once she had decided to make a meal, she ate and drank eagerly, suddenly aware that she was ravenously hungry. When she poured out her third glass of wine, she knew she was already mildly drunk. What does it matter, she thought, and tossed off the sweet white wine defiantly. It was better to learn her fate when her mind was blurred by the comforting fumes of alcohol.

Franz Johann snapped his fingers, a gleam of satisfaction appearing in his eyes, and Anna watched him warily as he walked to the main door of the room. He issued a string of commands to the lackey stationed in the hallway, but the instructions were incomprehensible to Anna Teresa, who had just noticed that the walls were developing an alarming tendency to sway gently in time with her breathing.

'Feed him . . . fresh clothes . . . water . . . guards . . .'

She closed her eyes, the terrible weariness of despair seeping into her limbs, leaving them heavy and languid. She buried her face in her hands and allowed exhaustion to carry her to the edges of sleep.

She was jerked back to consciousness by the barked commands and marching feet of a troop of soldiers. She opened her eyes and her startled gaze fell immediately upon a tall, broad-shouldered man surrounded by soldiers. He was pale but appeared relaxed, almost amused at the surroundings in which he found himself, until he saw Anna huddled in a corner of the room. His mouth tightened slightly before he turned away.

He was clothed entirely in black but he dominated the guards in their gaudy blue-and-yellow uniforms. His eyes burned fiercely against the arresting pallor of his face and his hair swept across his forehead in a dark, slashing line.

Inexplicable panic choked off all sounds in Anna's throat. She heard the clang of metal chain as the man moved towards Franz Johann and she wondered where it was coming from. The man halted, only inches from the Grand Duke.

'How good of you to ask me to call.' The man paused, a derisive smile twisting the corners of his hard mouth. 'Forgive me if I don't bow as I should. Circumstances, you know, sometimes prevent the proper courtesies.'

Anna's hypnotised gaze fixed itself on the man's arms. His hands, she saw, were shackled behind his back in a tangle of heavy iron.

Her cousin did not respond to the man's taunts. With a brief gesture he dismissed the guards. As soon as the soldiers left the room, he walked over to Anna's side and pulled her to her feet. He thrust her hands behind her back and forced her head round so that she faced the man in black.

'I have a pleasant surprise for you, Stefan,' he said. 'You are to be set free.'

Anna saw the leap of hope that flashed for one unguarded moment in the man's eyes. It was gone, almost before it came. 'I am gratified,' the man said sardonically. 'May I ask what secrets you are hoping I will betray in return for this generous offer of freedom?'

'No secrets, my dear Stefan. None. There is one

tiny condition of freedom, but I am sure you will discount it. I have somebody to introduce to you.' He jerked at Anna's elbows. 'This is Her Serene Highness, The Princess Anna Teresa. Make your bow to Stefan, my dear.'

Stefan and Anna stared at one another in incredulous silence and Franz Johann loosened his grip on her hands. He said, as if speaking to an idiot, 'Come, come, my dear. Haven't you learned your manners better than this? Princesses, you know, cannot be allowed to sulk. This gentleman is Stefan. Prince Stefan he is entitled to call himself these days. I'm afraid he was the leader of the rebels during our recent revolution. The hero of all the oppressed peasants. And he is soon to become your husband.'

Franz Johann chuckled and Anna felt a shiver of fear ripple down her spine. 'A crazy Prince for a mad Princess,' he said. 'Now was that not a brilliant idea of mine?'

CHAPTER
FIVE

Franz Johann's self-satisfied chuckles faded into silence and it was Stefan who finally broke the unnatural quiet in the room. Anna was beyond speech, almost beyond the point of coherent thought.

'Who is she?' Stefan asked curtly.

Franz Johann smiled. 'I told you. She says she is the Princess Anna Teresa.'

'We both know Anna Teresa is dead. Poor, innocent fool that she was.'

Franz Johann feigned astonishment. 'How can *you* possibly know any such thing, Stefan? Have you not been locked in a cell all day?'

'And have you still not learned that you cannot buy the loyalty of the people who are supposed to serve you? You can only earn it. Stone walls cannot prevent the free passage of information if there are no loyal servants to guard the walls.'

Franz Johann frowned, then settled back in his chair and sipped angrily at a glass of cognac. 'My dungeon walls, however, have kept your body safely incarcerated for the past three months.'

Stefan gestured impatiently. 'Let us stop playing word games, Franz. Who is this woman?'

'Who knows? By the time I . . . rescued . . . her from the soldiers of the castle guard, her wits were gone begging. Perhaps she is an Austrian spy. Yes, the more I think about it, the more likely it seems that she is an Austrian spy. The guards reported that she was trying to get into the castle to see me. They said she was desperate for an audience. Perhaps the Austrian authorities don't know I dislike women with her sort of voluptuous figure. The Austrian spy network has detoriated sadly, you know, since Metternich was forced out of office. In the old days, they would have trained their operatives better. This one couldn't stand the strain of even a few simple questions.'

Stefan's gaze flicked quickly over Anna's ripped gown. He looked at the cuts and grazes on her shoulders and the bruises marring her face. She saw scorn, followed by pity, reflected in his eyes before he turned abruptly away. It seemed to Anna that he couldn't bear to look at her any longer.

'I can't marry this woman,' he said, his voice empty of emotion. 'You know that I am pledged to marry Maria Muller.'

'Indeed, I know,' said Franz Johann and sipped some more of his cognac with evident satisfaction. 'Such terrible taste on your part, dear Stefan, to choose the daughter of a university professor who wastes his time churning out inflammatory political pamphlets. And poor Maria is so deplorably earnest. I met her once, at one of my father's receptions. Have you never found yourself just a trifle bored when in the good Miss Muller's company?'

'Unlike you, Franz, I do not require nightly orgies with young choirboys to keep me amused.'

'No, you are a pillar of rectitude, are you not? Except when you are inciting the Carthian people to revolution. Well, you have managed to attract a following among the ignorant peasants of this country and your continued absence from the Court is beginning to prove troublesome. There are some Councillors who listen to Professor Muller, and they are beginning to doubt that you are in Vienna as I have tried to pretend.'

'Are you admitting to me that your new crown sits a trifle unsteadily upon your head?' Stefan asked. He actually sounded amused, Anna thought, wishing she could understand the significance of their discussion.

Franz Johann scowled, but when he spoke, he had recovered his bland expression. 'You are too clever, Stefan, to believe I would consider setting you free unless I felt compelled to do so. I have decided that I must let you go, but I shall cut off your base of support by forcing you to marry this madwoman. Professor Muller may proclaim he is a republican, but I expect he is like every other *bourgeois*: he secretly loves the idea of his boring daughter marrying a prince. Even if you are a dubious prince of doubtful parentage. How long do you think your coalition of rebels would hold together, without Professor Muller to support you with his clever pamphlets? How high do you think your reputation will stand among the rebels when they find out you have bought your freedom by marrying a woman of my choice? A woman whom I shall declare is a leading member of the hated Austrian Imperial Court?'

'I shall not marry her, so I cannot say. I have grown quite attached to the comforts of my prison straw. It is certainly preferable to silken sheets shared with a mad Austrian woman.'

'You reach your decision too hastily, Stefan. I do not offer you the option of a return to your dungeon. You will marry this woman because if you do not, I shall kill you both. It will be a messy job, requiring a great many bribes, and I should prefer not to do it. But—believe me—I shall write the order for your execution tonight if you do not accept my conditions for freedom. I shall first order the execution of the madwoman, so that her death is on your conscience. Then I shall execute you.'

A small smile twisted the corners of the prisoner's mouth. 'You have never understood, have you Franz? You still don't realise that it is better to die honourably than to live with a guilty conscience.'

'How unendurably priggish you sometimes sound, Stefan. Let me remind you of one of the proverbs so well-loved by your peasant friends. *While there is life, there is hope.* I am taking a gamble in setting you free. I admit it openly. Why don't you decide to live and defeat me?'

Stefan laughed grimly. 'Almost, little brother, you tempt me. If I did not know you better, I would not even suspect there was some hidden trap to your apparent generosity.' He walked away from Franz Johann, turning his back towards them both. He was silent for so long that Anna, who could think of absolutely nothing rational to say, started to drift off into unconsciousness. She came to with a jolt when the prisoner jerked round with a sudden exclamation. He faced Franz Johann, his eyes cold with dislike.

'Very well,' he said. 'I will marry the woman. Not for the reasons you suggested, but for reasons of my own.'

Franz Johann smiled with satisfaction. 'Don't think I am ignorant of your motives in agreeing to the match. We both know that your death would spark another revolution among the peasantry. We both know I would succeed in crushing that rebellion. You fear for the lives and safety of your followers. I fear for my reputation with the Austrian Imperial Court. I wish to reassure them that the situation here is under control. You wish for your freedom. It is fortunate, is it not, that we both see your marriage as a way out of our dilemma?'

Stefan neither acknowledged nor denied the accuracy of Franz Johann's statement. He walked over to the corner where Anna Teresa sat huddled on the little satin-covered chair.

'What is your name?' he asked gently. 'Could you not trust me enough to tell me the truth?'

'I am the Princess Anna Teresa,' she mumbled, although she realised as soon as she had spoken that her answer simply condemned her as a madwoman in Stefan's eyes. 'I don't want to marry you,' she said with a brief flash of her old spirit. 'Who are you? Where do you come from?'

'I am Stefan of Innesbad,' he said. 'I am the younger brother of Franz Johann.'

The statement was so outrageous, it penetrated even Anna's weary and sleep-fuddled brain. 'Of course you are not,' she snapped. 'I would have met you if you were Franz Johann's brother. My parents never so much as mentioned your name.'

Franz Johann spoke quickly. 'She is remarkably convincing in her portrayal of the Princess Anna Teresa, is she not? I have been wondering whether she is truly mad, or merely stubborn.'

Anna felt anger flow through her tired body as

she heard her cousin's deceitful words. The anger
enabled her to find sufficient energy to set her brain
working once again. She looked at Franz Johann
without concealing her contempt, and it was he
who dropped his gaze first. She made no comment
on the lies he had told, for past experience warned
her that there would be no point.

'Why does this man claim he is your brother?' she
asked as calmly as she could.

'He is my half-brother,' Franz Johann replied
brusquely. 'We share the same mother, but I'm
afraid she was a flighty creature, notorious for her
lovers. Stefan was born ten months after my father
left for a tour of duty at the Austrian Imperial court
in Vienna. When he returned, my father banished
his wife from Innesbad and my bastard brother
grew up with his mother in exile. His early years
were spent in England, which no doubt explains
some of his extraordinary ideas about the correct
way to govern a country.'

Anna was sufficiently startled to address Stefan
directly. 'Why did you come back to Carthia?' she
said. 'Surely you would have done better pursuing
some career in England?'

Franz Johann spoke before his half-brother
could reply. His voice was hard with remembered
anger. 'My father's wits deserted him at the end of
his life. He summoned Stefan back to Innesbad
and made him his chief Councillor of State. He
issued documents giving Stefan the title of
Prince and lavished gifts and affection on him.
While I—his true son and heir—I was virtually
barred from the Court. Fortunately, my father died
in an accident before he could commit the ultimate
folly of publicly proclaiming Stefan's legitimacy.'

'Your father, the old Count, died only about four months ago,' Anna said slowly.

Stefan's smile taunted his brother. 'Yes, that's right, isn't it, Franz? Just about the time I was thrown into gaol. But you didn't succeed, did you? For all your careful planning, you don't know what my father spent his last moments writing. And the archbishop would never tell you what happened to the papers.'

Franz Johann's features contorted with hatred. 'By God, I'll find those documents! You're a bastard, do you hear? Nothing but a bastard!' With a visible effort at control, he lowered his voice and forced himself back into calmness. 'Besides, my dear Stefan, by the time you are married the meandering scrawls of my father's deathbed will be of no interest to anybody. The revolutionaries will never accept an Austrian as Grand Duchess. With this woman as your wife, you will be finished as a popular leader in Carthia.'

'You have no proof I am Austrian,' said Anna Teresa.

'But I shall have by tomorrow morning, my dear. I shall have several pages of written proof. You can count upon it.'

She sank down on the chair in helpless resignation. Defying her cousin was like fighting with a mist. The enemy dissolved in her grasp. She realised that Stefan was once more standing at her side and she stared into his grey eyes, hypnotised by the power she sensed whenever he was near. His gaze rested for a moment on her mouth and she was struck by the most extraordinary sensation, unlike anything she had ever felt before. Colour rushed into her cheeks and she lowered her lashes quickly, not wanting to betray the strange emotions struggling inside her.

'Are you willing to marry me?' Stefan asked. His voice was no longer gentle. In fact, it sounded harsh, almost angry. 'He will kill you, you know, if you don't agree.'

She gave a small, quivering laugh that ended in a sob. Even she recognised that it sounded very much like the laughter of a woman who was mentally unhinged. 'It is not much of a choice, is it? But I think I prefer marriage to death.'

'It is settled then.' He turned aside without looking at her again and she raised her eyes from their examination of the carpet. She followed Stefan's swift progress across the room, aware of the same, peculiar sensation which had afflicted her earlier. Perhaps, she thought, she was experiencing the lingering effects of too many glasses of wine.

'When do you propose to marry us off?' Stefan asked Franz Johann curtly.

'The late Duke and Duchess of Carthia will be buried tomorrow, along with my sweet murdered bride, the Princess Anna Teresa. I think in three days I shall be sufficiently recovered to face the prospect of observing somebody else's joy. And the populace should be ready for a minor celebration, don't you agree? I shall make a proclamation tomorrow. I shall announce that you have returned from Vienna and brought your bride with you. The ceremony . . . yes, I think the ceremony should be held in Innesbad Cathedral.'

'We are to have a very public wedding, I gather.'

'Oh very public, dear fellow. Very public. The Archbishop shall perform the ceremony and I shall call off the curfew. A generous gesture, don't you think?'

'Most generous,' said Stefan bitterly. 'The people of Carthia will certainly be left in no doubt at all that you approve of the marriage.'

'It is a clever touch,' Franz Johann agreed. 'And of course, the Dowager Grand Duchess won't be there, nor will the little Princess Luisa, so it will be understood that the more liberal elements of the old Court disapprove of the marriage. It is well thought out, is it not?'

'It shows all the hallmarks of your usual twisted thinking.'

Franz Johann bowed. 'A compliment from you, Stefan, is a compliment indeed.'

Stefan turned once more in Anna Teresa's direction, but he did not walk over to her side. 'Will you tell me your name?' he asked. 'If you do not, we shall be married without even that much basic honesty between us. Franz Johann will choose a name for you if you do not tell me yourself. Wouldn't you prefer the dignity of retaining your own true name?'

She drew in a deep breath and tried to make her voice sound eminently sane. How does a sane person sound in a world determined to consider her a lunatic, she wondered? 'Indeed, I should prefer to retain my own name and my own identity,' she said clearly. 'I am the Princess Anna Teresa of Carthia.'

Stefan shrugged his shoulders, not troubling to conceal his anger. 'I shall find out what name Franz Johann has chosen for you on our wedding-day. It will be soon enough for me. Goodnight, madam.'

Franz Johann beamed his approval of their disagreement. 'How very accommodating you are being, Stefan. I confess, I didn't expect such easy agreement. You have made me very happy.'

Stefan bowed ironically. 'It seems I am destined to serve you in innumerable ways, little brother.'

Franz Johann tugged at the golden bellrope and a footman hastened into the room.

'Send some soldiers to take the prisoner away.'

The footman bent almost double and backed himself out of the room still hunched into an obsequious bow. The soldiers arrived almost immediately. Presumably they had been waiting outside the door in case Stefan burst out of his chains and shackles and attempted to attack Franz Johann.

'The prisoner is not to be returned to his cell,' said Franz Johann to the officer in charge. 'Take him to the Purple suite of rooms in the West wing of the castle. He may order whatever food he wishes and he may send for fresh clothing, but he is never to go outside the rooms and he is never to be left alone. *Never!* Do I make myself crystal-clear?'

'Yes, Your Highness.'

The soldiers gathered around Stefan, enclosing his black figure within the flashing circle of their bright uniforms. He dominated them still, just as he had when he entered the Grand Duke's presence. He inclined his head to Franz Johann in a farewell gesture that stopped just sort of insolence.

'I am certainly touched by your generosity, little brother.'

'Get out! Take him away!'

The rattle of swords and the sound of leather-booted feet faded into the distance. Anna Teresa walked across the thick carpet to confront her cousin.

'Well, Franz, am I also to be given the privilege of a room where I can rest? It must be almost dawn, which means that it is close to twenty-four hours since I had any sleep.'

'Of course you may rest. I am not a monster. Even the mad may sleep while under my protection. Some serving-women shall be sent for. They shall protect you from the harmful consequences of your own insanity. So great is my generosity that I shall even provide a modest trousseau for you, mad though you are.'

'And my wedding-dress, Franz? Or has that been buried with my lady-in-waiting? I assume it is she who lies in the cathedral at Carlsberg?'

'I cannot conceive what you are talking about, my dear young lady. But certainly you shall have a pretty frock for your wedding. You deserve it.'

'It will not work, you know, Franz.'

'What will not work?'

'Whatever you are planning. The rebel leaders will realise Stefan did not want to marry me. He has only to tell them the truth.'

Franz Johann laughed softly. 'For the past two months and more I have cursed the strength that kept Stefan defiant where other men would have crumbled. Now the victory is mine. Stefan does not look like a man who has survived nearly three months of deprivation and torture.'

'You admit then, that he has been tortured?'

'Come, come, my dear. You should know me better than that. I would never admit to torturing anybody. But I daresay you can see from his complexion that it is some months since Stefan has seen daylight.'

The reality of that image was suddenly too much for Anna. 'I want to go to bed,' she said tiredly. 'Let me alone, Franz. I have endured all that I can bear for one day.'

'Certainly you may go to bed,' he said, tugging at the bell rope again. He sent the footman away to find some female servants. 'Make sure Frau Schiller is in charge,' he added as the footman left the room. 'Now let me think,' he said, examining Anna's tired face with a malicious gleam of pleasure. 'Elisabeth . . . Gretchen . . . Klara . . . Adèle . . . What shall I call you?'

'You could try Anna Teresa,' she said, unable to keep the bitterness from her voice.

'Tut, tut, woman, you should strive to curb these flashes of insanity. They can only do you harm.'

A tapping at the door heralded the arrival of four young serving-girls, escorted by a grim-looking woman of formidable size.

'Ah yes,' said Franz Johann with a glance of satisfaction. 'Frau Schiller, I am glad you were able to come so promptly.'

The woman creaked into a heavy curtsy. 'Yes, Your Highness. It's always a pleasure to know I am serving you.'

'Frau Schiller, I present to you the future bride of Prince Stefan of Innesbad. She is the Fräulein . . . er . . . Alexandra Marie von Waldstein. She will be in your charge until her wedding three days from now. You will, I know, take the very greatest care of her.'

'Certainly, Your Highness.' The woman did not so much as glance in Anna Teresa's direction, although she dropped another one of her awkward curtsys vaguely towards Anna's corner of the room. 'Follow me, Fräulein von Waldstein.'

Anna walked obediently to the group of servants who were really, as everybody in the room knew, her gaolers. She was too tired to care. Silently, with one last bitter glance in Franz Johann's direction, she followed Frau Schiller out of the room and into a new life as the Austrian spy, Alexandra Marie von Waldstein.

CHAPTER
SIX

THE young servant-girl tied a taffeta petticoat over Anna's horsehair crinoline. Six layers of silk and lace now weighted Anna's movements, but she hardly noticed the cumbersome yards of material. The tiers of lace falling over her head had brought back the painful memories she so badly wanted to repress, and she had to struggle to retain control of herself. The servants had probably heard rumours that she was mad; she would not scream and confirm their suspicions.

The image of her mother, blood spattered over her lacy petticoats, took Anna's mind in a compulsive grip and would not let go. She knew the colour drained from her cheeks and she felt herself sway. She covered her eyes with her hand, as if she could ward off the brutal, bloodstained memories.

'Are you all right, Miss? Have I tied your laces too tight?'

Anna forced back the nausea, thrusting the images aside with an almost physical effort. She would not—could not—think about the past. She needed all her energy to make plans for the future. She managed to produce a small smile for the serving-girl. There were some advantages, after all, to years of rigorous training.

'No, my laces are not too tight,' she said.

'Perhaps I am a little nervous. After all, it is my wedding-day.'

The maid gave a romantic sigh, undeterred by the grim, watching figure of Frau Schiller. 'Oh, Miss! He is so Handsome, Prince Stefan! He will make a wonderful husband. I am sure every girl in Carthia envies you today.'

'It is a fortunate bride who captures such a prize,' Anna said dryly. 'I wonder what I ever did to deserve such good fortune?'

The maid blushed and, taking Anna's questions quite literally, she bent down so that Frau Schiller could not hear what was said. 'You're so beautiful, Miss. I believe Prince Stefan fell in love with you at first sight, whatever the others say. I don't believe he would betray our cause . . .' The maid gasped as she realised the damning extent of her indiscretion, and hurried away to start unwrapping Anna's muslin-shrouded wedding-dress.

Anna had no chance to reply, and in any case would not have spoken. There was no longer room in her life for moments of unguarded sympathy or little acts of kindness towards a maid. For the past three days she had had plenty of time to think as she paced the luxurious prison where Franz Johann kept her confined. She had had more than enough time to remember with horror the brutal details of her parents' assassination. She was confident after three nights of lonely weeping and wrenching nightmares, that she had no emotion left within herself save hatred for Franz Johann who had betrayed everything dear to her. Only a burning desire to avenge her parents' murders made each day seem worth living. She would marry Prince Stefan because by marrying him she could stay alive

long enough to plot her revenge against Franz
Johann. She would probably have married Satan
himself, if he could have guaranteed punishment
for Franz Johann.

It required three maids to lift the wedding-dress
over her head. It fell in soft folds of satin over the
stiff lace of her petticoats. In deference to the
official court mourning there was no decoration of
the white fabric. The maids adjusted the natural
pleats so that the skirt billowed out from Anna's
tiny waist. It took fifteen minutes to fasten the
satin-covered buttons that closed the back of the
gown.

She watched, but only with half her attention, as
the maid climbed on to little footstools to secure
her veil to her hair, and she wondered what they
would think if they could see inside her mind and
read the angry schemes for vengeance that chased
through her thoughts.

At last a maid gave a final adjustment to the
white ribbons of Anna's sash. 'It's all finished,
Miss,' she said. She spoke again, more loudly, so
that Frau Schiller would hear. 'Prince Stefan's
bride is ready.'

Anna immediately turned to look at herself in
the wall mirror, so that she could avoid meeting
Frau Schiller's eyes. Her cousin and Frau Schiller
were two of a kind, Anna thought. They both
derived positive pleasure from witnessing other
people's pain.

It was a tall, slender stranger who stared at her
from the glass, but Anna was not surprised. These
days she scarcely expected to recognise her own
reflection; she seemed to change every time she
looked in a mirror. This girl—it was difficult to call

her Anna—was pale-cheeked and had worried, dark blue eyes. Some of her thick hair had been draped in soft waves to cover the bruise that still marked her forehead. The remainder had been clustered in a mass of chestnut curls at the nape of her neck. Her white throat looked almost too fragile to support the weight of her hair. The veil, thrown back from her face, blurred the outlines of her body, emphasising her appearance of shadowy fragility. The girl looked, Anna decided, delicate and insubstantial, not a very enticing bride. At least she didn't look like a madwoman and that was victory enough for the time being.

Her self-inspection was interrupted by a flurry of activity behind her. She turned round with deliberate slowness to find Franz Johann staring at her. Reluctantly, hating herself because she felt the need to conform, she bent her knees in a tiny curtsy. As the new Grand Duke of Carthia, he was entitled to such a gesture from everybody, even Princess Anna Teresa.

She rose quickly, her head held high, and for a moment she glimpsed a flash of annoyance in Franz Johann's eyes. It was quickly concealed.

He covered his face with his hand and allowed his voice to break on a smothered sob. 'Ah, it is too much! I shouldn't have pushed myself to attend Prince Stefan's wedding when all my own hopes of happiness lie buried in the cold ground.'

'You should strive to resurrect your hopes, Your Highness. Who can guess how quickly another Princess Anna Teresa may be found?'

His body stiffened for an instant, but it was quickly relaxed again. 'There can *never* be another Princess Anna Teresa,' he said firmly. 'Are you ready to leave for the cathedral, Fräulein von Waldstein? I personally am to give your hand in marriage to Prince Stefan.'

'I am deeply honoured.'

Franz Johann smiled his gratification, completely ignoring her sarcasm. 'There is almost nothing I would not do to see you and Prince Stefan happily wed. Only think! When next these good servants see you, you will be a Princess. What a change in your position to be sure! Come, my dear Fräulein, we must not keep the Archbishop of Carthia waiting.'

An old-fashioned gilded coach was drawn up at the main entrance to the castle. Franz Johann stepped into the red-velvet interior, then waited for Anna to seat herself opposite him. There was a sound of shouted commands from the guard of mounted soldiers and the cavalcade rode out from the courtyard.

She would not think about her last coach journey, Anna told herself. She would *not* remember it. She forced her mind into a state of blankness, then stared out of the window although she saw nothing of the passing scene. Her eyes were blinded by unshed tears, but she held her shoulders rigidly erect, and schooled her mouth into a tiny smile. They were almost at the cathedral before she realised that the streets were lined with people who viewed the passage of the golden coach in grim silence. The town was so quiet that Anna could hear the jingle of the soldiers' spurs and the rattle of the coach wheels as they drove over the cobbled roads.

She brought her gaze back from the silent streets and glanced across the carriage at Franz Johann.

His mouth was clamped into a straight line but, with a perceptiveness that would have been alien to her nature only a week earlier, Anna knew that he could scarcely contain his satisfaction. He was prepared to tolerate this sign of dislike from the Carthian people, providing he could taint his half-brother with the same unpopularity.

The carriage halted outside the cathedral entrance. Trumpets delivered a fanfare to herald their arrival. Franz Johann stepped out of the carriage and graciously assisted Anna Teresa to descend. Two small page-boys lifted the corners of her train and together they mounted the cathedral steps. At least the blaring music masked the continued silence of the crowds.

The trumpets fell silent as they entered the cathedral and immediately the great organ burst forth with the sounds of the Carthian national anthem. Her wedding ceremony could not have been more splendid, Anna thought ironically, if it had been arranged to unite a king and a queen instead of a bastard prince and a supposed mad-woman.

Franz Johann had arranged her veil over her face, which made it difficult for the guests to discern the outline of her features. Not that he need have worried about recognition. Anna Teresa had reached the point where she felt so unlike the young, spoiled, pampered girl who had set out for the hunting lodge, that she doubted if her own mother could have recognised her. But the veil made it easier to conceal her emotions. Behind its safe anonymity she could pretend it was somebody else who walked down the aisle towards marriage with a former revolutionary leader. The real Anna

Teresa, she consoled herself, was not present in the cathedral.

Her steady pace down the long aisle faltered only once, when she accidentally allowed her gaze to focus for a minute on the tall, intimidating figure who stood waiting at one side of the high altar. Although she had met Stefan under such extraordinary circumstances, she recognised him instantly, even from a distance of thirty yards. For a second her heart seemed to stop beating, then it rushed on again, faster than before. Determinedly, she recovered her step and walked smoothly down the remainder of the aisle.

She knew the Archbishop, of course. He had confirmed her when she was a child and had officiated at many state functions over the past fifteen years. For a wild moment she wondered what he would do if she flung back her veil and announced that she was the Princess Anna Teresa. She did not pursue the thought, because she could guess what would happen without putting the Archbishop to the test. He wouldn't recognise her. After all, he had buried the Princess Anna Teresa in the cathedral at Carlsberg only three days previously. Her gesture would achieve nothing and the crowd of guests would be witnesses to a scene that certified her as insane. Had Franz Johann hoped for just such a doomed appeal to the Archbishop? She shuddered at the thought, chilled by the realisation that she had nothing with which to defend herself now save her own wits. She was no longer a princess; she no longer had a family and friends to protect her.

She felt Franz Johann take her icy-cold hand and place it in Stefan's clasp. The choir started singing,

and the Archbishop began to chant the familiar
opening to the wedding service. Stefan's hand felt
warm through the thin silk of her glove. His arm
was rock-firm, and if she had not known such
kindness was impossible, she would have thought
he was offering her support. Perhaps he was. What
else could he do with a wife he believed to be mad,
except try to support and control her?

'I, Alexandra Marie . . .' She heard the soft
words and could scarcely believe it was her own
voice that responded so obediently to the
Archbishop's prompting. 'I promise to love . . . to
honour . . . to obey . . .' Why was she accepting
the false identity Franz had thrust upon her? *I am
the Princess Anna Teresa*, she wanted to scream.
Franz Johann, your new Grand Duke is an assassin.
Why didn't she cry out the truth? Because I want to
live, came the cynical response from somewhere
deep inside her. Because I will not let Franz Johann
escape punishment for what he has done to my
family.

She felt Stefan remove her finger from her glove,
which was already slit along an inner seam. His
voice was steady and faintly hard as he repeated the
false words of undying love and devotion. He
pushed the heavy gold band over her slender finger
and she quivered involuntarily at his touch. She
looked up, unable to prevent the instinctive movement, and found Stefan's gaze fixed upon her.
The breath-catching sensations she had experienced before in his company returned and
made her tremble. I am married, she thought in-
credulously, and looked at the Archbishop so that
she would not have to look into Stefan's cold grey
eyes.

The Archbishop murmured a blessing. The choristers burst into song. The wedding was over. She wanted to laugh at the irony of it all. She wanted to cry. But she couldn't allow herself the luxury of either tears or laughter and so she remained silent, her features schooled to impassivity.

She walked back down the aisle of the cathedral, escorted by her husband. Together she and Stefan came out of the dimness of the church into the brilliant light of the mid-day sun. Many people were still gathered in the cathedral square, and they were as silent as ever.

Prince Stefan surveyed the crowds and flashed a mocking smile at his half-brother. 'What a popular Grand Duke you are proving to be, Franz old fellow.' His voice was deceptively mild, but Anna could feel the muscles of his arm tighten beneath her hand. She must have made some involuntary movement, for Stefan looked down at her as if he had just remembered her presence and she could see the anger which tensed his body and constricted his breathing.

'At least I can make the people believe I have betrayed them for love and not for political gain,' he muttered. With a swift movement that took her by surprise, he lifted the tip of her veil and pushed it away from her face. Astonishment swept over his features until, with an almost imperceptible shake of his head, he resumed his mask of cold, angry indifference. He pulled Anna into his arms and pressed her face against his cheek. To the onlookers, it must have seemed that they exchanged a passionate embrace. A ragged cheer came from the crowd and Stefan waved his hand in friendly acknowledgement.

'Smile!' he hissed at Anna. 'Look at me and smile!'

She obeyed, because the habit of obedience to authority was deeply engrained. She was the Princess Anna Teresa, and she had been trained to smile even when her heart was breaking. As she responded to another burst of cheering from the crowd, she wondered why she had obeyed a man who was a traitor and a revolutionary. Prince Stefan she reminded herself, had led the rebellion against her father. It would be dangerous to fall into the habit of thinking him an ally, just because Franz Johann had imprisoned him. Even her desire to bring Franz Johann to justice could not justify co-operating with a revolutionary.

There was no banquet following the wedding ceremony. Franz Johann explained the absence of a formal reception by reminding the guests of his recent bereavement and the official state of mourning in Carthia. After making a short speech, he proceeded at once to his royal carriage, leaving Stefan and Anna to follow in his wake. A troop of soldiers made sure that they went in the direction Franz Johann had indicated.

They completed the journey without exchanging a single word. Anna was determined she was not going to be the first one to break the silence. She had no idea what she would do when they arrived back at the castle, but the dilemma was resolved for her since they were greeted by another detachment of the Grand Duke's personal bodyguard.

'I am to escort you to the Grand Duke Franz Johann's private chambers, Your Excellencies,' said the Captain of the Guard.

'What an *unexpected* pleasure,' Stefan said.

The Captain bowed. If he had understood Stefan's irony he gave no sign. 'Follow me, please, Your Excellencies.' To make sure his request was not ignored, the troop of soldiers surrounded Anna and Stefan so that they had no choice other than to obey. Within a very few minutes, they were in Franz Johann's private apartment and the bodyguards had been dismissed.

'So . . .' Franz Johann remarked. 'A very handsome couple you make to be sure. And a delightful wedding, even if it is immodest of me to praise the arrangements. Will you join me in a glass of champagne?'

'We are neither of us in the mood for glasses of champagne, Franz. If you will call off your battalions of soldiers, we should like to leave Innesbad.'

'Already you speak of your wife and yourself as one! Is it possible that I have precipitated a love match?'

'I asked if we are to be allowed to leave,' Stefan repeated, ignoring his brother's jibe. 'Or have you already decided to break your promises?'

'My dear fellow, why should I dream of preventing you from leaving? Why should I wish to detain such impetuous young lovers at Innesbad? Your own carriage and four of your horses await you in the western courtyard. I ordered them myself.'

'And my servants? Do they await me also?'

'You servants, I'm afraid, are not in a condition to be of any further use to you. Obstinate creatures most of them. But I have supplied you with grooms from my own household, and you will find some of my servants waiting for you at your house. You will be admirably served, I guarantee it.'

'I'm sure you do.' Stefan turned away, not

bothering to mask his impatience. For the first time since their encounter on the cathedral steps, he spoke directly to Anna although he still did not look at her. 'Are you ready to leave, madam? It is late afternoon, we should be on our way.'

'Of course I'm not ready,' she protested. 'I must change my clothes. I cannot ride around the countryside in a wedding-dress!'

'Why not?' he asked indifferently. 'It covers you quite adequately, and I will provide you with a cloak if you fear the evening chill. I would prefer not to delay more than necessary. I wish to reach . . . our stopping-place . . . before nightfall.'

She wanted to defy him and insist on changing her clothes, but she would not give Franz Johann the satisfaction of witnessing an argument. 'It shall be as you wish,' she said evenly. She turned to face her cousin. 'Goodbye, Franz. Whatever may transpire in the future, today has at least brought me one unsurpassable benefit.'

'What is that, my dear *Princess*?'

'I don't have to marry you,' she said.

Franz Johann pulled at the bellrope, obviously angry for having given her the opportunity to insult him. 'Take your mad wife away, Stefan. She is beginning to annoy me.' He saw that the commanding officer of the bodyguard had stepped into the room and he gave a curt order. 'Escort Prince Stefan and his bride to the main west courtyard. They are leaving Innesbad.'

'Yes, Your Highness.'

Franz Johann picked up his glass of champagne, staring morosely into its depths. 'Stefan!' he said, just as Anna and her new husband reached the door of the room.

'. . . Your Highness?'

'You are banished to your estate in Styrweld,' Franz Johann said. 'If you, or your wife, try to leave the estate, you will both be executed. Don't try to persuade the coachdriver to take you anywhere else. They have their orders.'

Stefan studied his half-brother in silence, then laughed with apparently genuine humour. 'So that is how you hope to do it,' he said. 'So conveniently legal. But have you considered the possibility that I may not need to leave the estate?'

Franz Johann's eyes burned with hatred. 'The documents cannot be there. We have searched every inch of the property. This time I am going to win, Stefan. Sooner or later, you will leave the estate to retrieve those papers, and I will have you. My father was insane when he wrote them, do you hear me? He was mad with pain, mad!'

'The priest declared he was entirely sane,' Stefan said. 'The Archbishop has declared in public that my father was in full possession of his faculties on the day that he died.'

Two spots of colour burned high on Franz Johann's cheeks. 'He was not your father! You're a bastard and no priest will be able to change that!' The hectic flush faded from his cheeks and his voice was under control when he spoke again. 'It doesn't matter what that senile Archbishop tries to say. Everybody knows he is the next best thing to a declared revolutionary. Anyway, now he has married you to a hated Austrian woman, perhaps he won't be so anxious to support your claims. Who will follow you now that you have sided with our Imperial rulers? What peasant will trust you? I am even looking forward to reading Professor Muller's next pamphlet. It should make entertaining reading.'

Somehow Anna could sense the frustration that gripped Prince Stefan, although not a trace of emotion showed on his face.

'Send me a copy in exile,' he said, his voice sounding light and uncaring. 'I will let you know just how entertaining I find it. You may discover that Professor Muller is not as easily fooled as you imagine.' Without changing his voice or manner in any way, he spoke to Anna.

'Come, madam. It is time for us to go.'

CHAPTER
SEVEN

ONE of the servants had procured a light woollen cloak, and Stefan threw it over her shoulders as they stepped out of the castle into the sunlit courtyard. He did not look at her—in fact, he had scarcely glanced in her direction since that moment outside the cathedral—and his profile remained arrogant and aloof.

Anna watched him covertly as he had a brief discussion with the groom. There was no warmth in his manner of speaking to the servant, but this was not one of his own lackeys, and anyone working for Franz Johann was certain to be a spy.

It was an odd sensation to look at the stranger who was now her husband, seeing for the first time how his thick, dark hair curled slightly at the nape of his neck, noticing the latent strength of his tall, slender body. When he moved, it was with a powerful, leashed elegance, as though the clothes he wore hid a physical force kept under rigid control. Her gaze travelled up to his mouth, which was well-shaped but set in a cold, uncompromising line. He turned suddenly, and she dropped her long lashes to hide her eyes. She would never let him see that he held the slightest interest for her. He was her enemy, even if not quite as implacable a one as Franz Johann.

'We are ready to leave if you will enter the carriage,' he said. He offered his arm with a formal courtesy that underlined his complete absence of feeling.

Anna took his proffered arm and felt once again the hard muscles beneath the smooth velvet of his coat. She shivered inwardly. She had managed to escape death at Franz Johann's hands, but she was not at all certain that her fate with Stefan was any more promising. What did she know about him save that he was a revoluntionary and a bastard by birth? She reflected as she settled herself in a corner of the carriage that her husband would be a dangerous enemy.

They were scarcely seated before the grooms whipped up the horses and the carriage left the courtyard at a spanking pace. As soon as they reached the open road, the groom gave the lead horse its head and the coach rattled forward at breakneck speed.

Anna closed her eyes so that she would not have to watch the swaying landscape flash past the carriage windows. For a while she concentrated on praying that she would not be sick. Stefan made no inquiry as to how she felt. He continued to sit in stony silence even though she suspected that her complexion had faded to a delicate shade of green. Anna began to change her prayers. It would give her the greatest satisfaction, she thought angrily, if she could become violently ill. Preferably all over Stefan.

After an hour of unremitting speed, she could tolerate the violent jolting of the carriage no longer. 'Would you open the window?' she asked. She had wanted to sound icily remote, but sickness gripped her throat and her voice ended on a choked plea for air.

She was aware of his gaze flickering over her assessingly, although she kept her eyes closed. 'The dust will blow into the carriage,' he said.

'I'm wearing a veil. You will recall that I was given no chance to remove it after our wedding ceremony.' She pulled it across her face as she finished speaking.

He said nothing, ignoring her caustic tone of voice. She heard him lean forward and release the heavy leather strap that controlled the functioning of the window. A rush of fresh air fanned her cheeks, and she gulped it in gratefully.

'Are you going to be ill?' he asked the question brusquely, as though reluctant to express even that minimal amount of personal concern.

'No.' She still did not open her eyes. She could be as curt and unresponsive as he was.

'The servants have been given orders by my brother not to stop until we reach my estates,' he said. 'They would not obey me even if I ordered them to slow down. In fact, it would give them pleasure to think you are uncomfortable. In the circumstances, I trust you will be able to maintain your good health for another couple of hours.'

'Where are your estates?' Anna asked. She had not meant to speak, but the question slipped out before she could prevent it. After all, one of his estates was to be her home for the foreseeable future.

'The major part of my land lies in the north-west corner of Carthia. Styrweld is a hunting-lodge that was given me by the old Count of Innesbad. It is quite close to Bavaria.'

'Near Bavaria? Then your land lies closer to the German states than to the Austrian Empire,' Anna remarked.

'Yes.' His voice became even colder than before. 'You will be somewhat cut off from your Austrian masters, I'm afraid.'

At last she turned her gaze so that she looked at him directly. Her eyes flashed defiance and she kept her voice soft, but very clear. 'I am not Austrian,' she said. 'I am Carthian.'

'I know. You are the Princess Anna Teresa resurrected from the grave.'

She sighed, and leaned back against the dusty squabs of the carriage. She noticed that the upholstery smelled musty, as if it had been some months since the carriage was last used. She pressed her face into the cushioned corner of her seat, not caring about the damp smell. What was the point of talking to a man who would not even accept that she was telling the truth about the country of her birth? It was an exercise in futility for both of them. She could feel the nagging ache in her head expand into a pounding pain, but she was determined to make no more pleas to Stefan's non-existent generosity.

'Do you . . . Would you like me to remove either your train or your veil? You must feel uncomfortable sitting in such cumbersome garments.' There was no mistaking the reluctance with which Stefan made this offer of assistance, and a faintly bitter smile twisted Anna's mouth.

'Are you afraid I may faint? Don't be. I have worn many more unwieldy outfits.'

'I merely wished to relieve you of some unnecessary discomfort.'

'Your good manners are in perpetual conflict with your true feelings, are they not? It must go against the grain to be saddled with the care of a madwoman.'

'It would be better for all of us if I believed you to be truly mad,' Stefan said harshly. 'At least then I could consign you to the care of kindly nurses and hope for an improvement in your condition.' He made a brief, dismissing gesture with his hand. 'Enough. We will not speak of it, but if you wish to play the madwoman with conviction, you will have to do something about your eyes. They do not flash insanity.' Almost to himself he muttered, 'Believe me, they do no such thing.'

She was momentarily nonplussed by his response. She had been so sure that he thought her mad. She spoke uncertainly. 'I would like you to take off my train and my wedding veil. You were quite right; they are uncomfortable.'

Once again he said nothing. He came and sat beside her, slipping the cloak from her shoulders so that he could unhook the dozens of tiny fastenings that held her train to the shoulder seams of her wedding gown. His fingers accidentally brushed the nape of her neck and she pulled away sharply. Neither of them made any comment.

It was a long time before all the hooks were undone and Stefan placed the train on the seat beside her. It seemed to Anna that there was a faint flush along his high cheekbones that had not been there before. He did not look at her, but neither did he return to his own side of the carriage.

Anna didn't understand why her breathing was suddenly constricted, or why she wanted Stefan—her father's enemy—to turn and look at her.

'Aren't you going to remove my veil?' she asked. Her hands were shaking slightly as she lifted the white lace, pushing it away from her face. 'It will be easy for you to take off,' she said. 'But I couldn't find the pins without tearing the lace.' Her lips felt dry, and she moistened them with the tip of her tongue, aware that Stefan's eyes were fixed upon her mouth and that their normal grey colour had darkened to a deeper shade. She was shocked to feel a tiny thrill of pleasure ripple through her body.

They were both still for a moment, then she felt his fingers pulling out the silver clips, tugging sharply at a hairpin tangled in one of her curls. He completed the task in grim silence.

'Where do you want me to put the pins?' he asked curtly, when the veil was finally removed.

'Keep them.' She cleared her throat, determined to make her voice sound cool and efficient once again. 'I have no reticule,' she added in explanation.

He tucked the jewelled pins inside the pocket of his waistcoat without comment. 'We will see about providing you with some clothes when we reach Styrweld,' he said as he returned to his own side of the carriage.

'Thank you. I should prefer not to wear the ones Franz Johann provided.'

'What am I supposed to call you?' he asked when they had both spent several minutes staring out of their respective windows. 'Do you wish me to use the name Franz Johann gave you? What was it . . . Alexandra?'

'No,' she said. 'I don't want to be called Alexandra.'

'What then?'

Defiantly, she met his gaze. 'Anna,' she said. 'I wish you to call me Anna, because it's my name.'

She was frightened by the scorn that hardened his features, removing all colour from his grey eyes so that they swept over her with chilling, icy rage.

'You may not be mad,' he said. 'But you are a fool.'

Anna was filled with a rage of her own. She was sick of being a puppet who was forced to dance in response to her cousin's lies. 'Why are you so anxious to trust Franz Johann?' she asked. 'Why do you persist in believing I am Austrian? If it is too much for you to believe that I am the Princess Anna Teresa, haven't you learned yet that when your half-brother says something, it's wiser to believe the opposite? If he claims I am an Austrian spy, isn't that good reason for you to believe me when I say that I am not?'

The chill vanished from Stefan's eyes, to be replaced with a hint of wry humour. 'I did not think there could be any argument to persuade me that you are not the enemy spy that you seem. You are a brilliant woman, my dear. You have found the only argument which can force me to doubt the evidence of my own eyes.'

Anna Teresa did not attempt to conceal her bewilderment. 'What do you mean? What have I done to convince you I am a spy?'

Stefan's laughter was harsh, no longer even faintly amused. 'You are doing it again, my dear. That marvellous act of hurt innocence. Your eyes swim with unshed tears, your lips tremble on the verge of a sob. And then, as soon as I am idiotic enough to respond to your wiles, your eyes send me quite a different message. They promise me every joy a woman can give to a man, if only I will be fool enough to surrender.'

Anna's bewilderment increased. 'I have never promised you anything,' she said uncertainly. 'Except in the cathedral, when we were both of us lying. How could I make you promises? We have hardly spoken to one another.'

'Your promises were not made with words, madam. They were made with the movements of your body, and the flashes of your eyes. I have a long experience with women who are trying to gain my confidence merely to betray it. You will not find me an easy victim.'

She was given no opportunity to reply. The silence of the early evening was shattered by a burst of rifle fire and the carriage momentarily slowed before rushing forward, out of control. Anna saw the body of the coach-driver topple from the carriage and fall with a sickening thud on the dirt road.

She heard a woman scream, a high-pitched hysterical scream that was a brutal echo of the attack upon her parents. She felt the sting of Stefan's hand slash across her cheek and she realised that this time she was the woman screaming. Stefan pulled her into his arms, forcing her down on the floor of the carriage, and thrusting his body on top of hers. Every movement seemed to be the repetition of a familiar nightmare. The velvet of his jacket pressed against her nostrils and something inside her brain snapped. She tossed her head in wild, terrified movements, drumming her heels on the carriage floor in a desperate, futile effort to break free. She scarcely heard the pounding hoofs of the horses galloping alongside the carriage and regaining control, but when the door was wrenched open she gave up the useless struggle against Stefan. Just before panic blackened her mind, she thought she heard him say, 'Thank God! You came!' Her body gave one last, convulsive movement, then she allowed herself to slip into the welcome darkness of oblivion.

It was the smell of freshly-brewed coffee which awakened her. At first she was aware only of the comforting smell, then gradually she noticed that her body ached, and at last she became aware of voices all around her.

She was afraid to open her eyes, afraid of what new danger might be waiting to greet her once she allowed herself to become fully conscious. She moved very slightly and found she was lying on some sort of truckle-bed, primitive but well-provided with cushions. Cautiously, she opened her eyes. There were five men in the room. Her eyes flickered over the group until she identified Stefan's tall, powerful frame, and immediately some of the tension in her body drained away. She did not pause to wonder why that should be.

None of the men paid any attention to her, so she moved even more cautiously than before, seeking a better view of the men. She was fairly certain that she made no sound, but Stefan's gaze moved fractionally and for a second his eyes locked with hers. He looked away again, not betraying by so much as a quiver that he was aware of her return to consciousness. She wondered why he didn't mention to the men that she was awake. Were the men his friends? What had been happening while she was lying on the truckle-bed, oblivious to the world around her?

A short, stout man pounded his fist on the table, making Anna's head throb with renewed pain. She forced herself to ignore the ache and to listen to what the man was saying.

'We had reached a settlement with the old Duke, it's true. But there's no way we can trust the new Grand Duke to keep to the terms of that agreement. Already the few gains we made have been reversed: public meetings are forbidden; the Professor's printing presses have been destroyed; the promises the old Duke made have been broken. And you are telling us, Stefan, that we should put away our arms and stop fighting for the freedom of our people! Despite the rumours Franz Johann has circulated about you, I told the others you would never turn traitor to our cause. But Stefan, old friend, you must justify the statements you have made tonight.'

When he replied, Stefan's voice sounded calm. Anna wondered if anybody besides herself guessed he was nowhere near as impassive as he appeared. She wasn't even sure how she had managed to divine his inner tension.

'Our cause may be just, Georg,' Stefan said quietly, 'but that doesn't mean victory lies within our grasp. The revolutionary tide is receding all over Europe. The Hungarians are defeated, Kossuth is in exile, the new Parliament in Frankfurt bickers among its own members instead of uniting in opposition to the imperial powers. Can't you see that this is no moment to risk the lives of the Carthian people in a futile uprising against Franz Johann? If the Austrians did not march against us, the Prussians would. You must give me time to think of a different course of action, more subtle than the use of peasants as cannon-fodder for Franz Johann's troops.'

Another of the men, young and thin and wearing the traditional garb of a Carthian University student, strode to the centre of the room, his voice shaking with passion as he began to speak. 'I see only that you have turned traitor while you were in the Grand Duke's power. What methods did he use to corrupt you? Was it the torture you could not stand, or was it the promise of a luscious woman from the Austrian court which proved irresistible? We all know who your wife was: she was the favourite of the Austrian Emperor and given to you as a special reward.'

There was an immediate stirring of protest in the small group gathered round the table. Anna closed her eyes, knowing that more than one of the men glanced towards her as the student finished speaking. Georg intervened hastily, his face suffused with an embarrassed flush.

'Hans does not mean what he says, Stefan. He knows—we all know—how bravely you withstood the threats of torture and the starvation Franz Johann subjected you to.'

'Do you?' Stefan's profile was chilling and remote as Anna had ever seen it. 'Even you, Georg, have questioned my motives. Hans openly doubts my courage and he claims I can be corrupted simply by the promise of a pretty girl to share my bed. If you all suspect that my dedication to the cause of freedom is no longer as great as it once was, I can only tell you that you are wrong. If you do not understand me well enough to know that I could never betray beliefs that have been instilled in me since early boyhood, then there are no proofs I can offer which would serve to convince you of my desire to see Carthia established as an independent and democratic nation.'

The general murmur of approval was interrupted by the student Hans. 'That is all very well; we know you are a clever orator, Prince Stefan. If you are so dedicated to the cause of the common people, then why did you marry that woman . . . that Austrian creature chosen by Franz Johann and the Emperor of Austria to spy upon us? I suggest that we kill her now and save ourselves a great deal of trouble later.'

'I would remind you that you are speaking of my *wife*. Do you believe that I have become so feeble-minded in captivity that I would bring an Austrian spy into your midst?'

Hans scarcely concealed a sneer, although the other men were looking uncomfortable once again. 'She is beautiful enough to tempt any man to treachery. She certainly caused you to break your word of honour to the daughter of Professor Muller, who has done so much for the Carthian people.'

'That is enough, Hans!' The man Georg moved forward decisively to break up the confrontation. 'Our cause is just and we do not kill people because they are unknown to us. Stefan is the guarantee of his own wife's loyalty, as I guarantee the loyalty of my wife and daughters. It is not for you to question Stefan's marriage.'

Stefan placed his hand on Georg's arm. 'Thank you, but perhaps Hans only expresses doubts which you all share,' he said quietly. He walked away from the table and poured himself a cup of coffee from the pot warming on the hob. He didn't look at Anna. 'When Professor Muller arrives I will explain my actions to him privately. He may tell you whatever he wishes. I think, until I have spoken to Professor Muller, it is sufficient to say that I was forced by circumstances beyond my control to break my commitment to Maria Muller. I bitterly regret my betrayal of Maria's trust, but that does not make me a traitor to our political cause.'

There was a silence in the room. It was easy for Anna to guess that the men gathered in this small farmhouse were revolutionary leaders of the recent rebellion. She ought to feel little sympathy for their problems and none at all for Stefan. What did it matter to her if a group of rebels decided Stefan was a traitor? She heard the men start to mutter among themselves and, to her astonishment, she found her hands were wet with nervous tension. Without stopping to question her own motives, she got up from the narrow truckle-bed and walked quickly into the centre of the room.

'Prince Stefan hasn't told you the complete truth,' she said in a low, clear voice. The men stared at her, too surprised to speak, stunned into silence by her unexpected intrusion into their debate. She glanced briefly towards the hearth so that she could look at Stefan. His grey eyes raked over her with a sardonic gleam that scarcely concealed the anger lurking close to the surface. He clearly expected her to undermine his position in any way that she could. She turned away from his accusing eyes and spoke quickly to the other men.

'Prince Stefan endured great pain and near starvation rather than reveal your names to Franz

Johann,' she said. 'I saw him when he was still a prisoner in the Innesbad dungeons, and I know that his captivity was cruelly enforced. I also know that the Grand Duke ultimately gave up his attempts to break Prince Stefan's spirit. He realised that Stefan would die before he revealed any useful information to Franz Johann's torturers.'

'What has this got to do with his reasons for marrying you?' Hans asked. 'How do we know that you're not defending him for your own good reasons?'

'Prince Stefan is too considerate of my feelings to explain exactly why he married me. He broke his promise to Miss Muller in order to save my life. The Grand Duke threatened to execute me, if Stefan would not marry me.'

She saw the surprise, swiftly followed by wariness, that chased across Stefan's features.

'Is this true, Stefan?' Georg asked. 'Your wife was yet another of Franz Johann's victims?'

'It is true that her life was threatened,' Stefan replied stiffly. 'But she makes too much of my generosity. Franz Johann threatened my life as well as hers if we did not marry.' He gestured impatiently with his hand. 'My wife must be exhausted, gentlemen, and hungry as well. You can see that she has not even had time to change out of her wedding-gown. She suffered a considerable shock when your men attacked our carriage. Could we not be left alone with each other until Professor Muller arrives? We can take no final decisions on our future plans until the Professor is here.'

'I think that would be best,' Georg agreed. 'The revolution will not be lost because we take time to eat some supper. I will send my daughter in with

food for you both. Stefan . . .' He bowed slightly in
the direction of the Prince, then hesitated before
executing a similar bow before Anna Teresa.
'Please make yourselves comfortable, Your Excellencies. You will have supper shortly.'

'Thank you Georg.' Stefan waited until all sound
of footsteps faded into silence. He went back to the
fire, poured coffee into a pottery mug and handed it
to Anna. 'Here,' he said. He waited while she
sipped gratefully at the steaming liquid. 'Why did
you come to my defence?' he asked quietly.

Anna twisted her wedding-ring nervously
around her finger. It was too big, she noticed. As
soon as she realised what she was doing, she stopped and thrust her hands behind her back. 'I don't
know,' she said at last.

'I . . . appreciate your help. Thank you.'

She could not bear it when he spoke to her in
such a gentle voice. She had to remember that he
was the enemy. She forced herself to shrug her
shoulders. 'There is no point in allowing those men
to distrust you. *My* position is hardly improved if
they should decide to murder you.'

Stefan's face lost it gentleness. 'I am glad you
appreciate the realities of your position. May I take
it that you are prepared to work with me to convince my colleagues that I am still to be trusted?'

'Why should I?'

'You have already given one very good reason. If
they do not trust me, *you* may not leave here alive.'

She laughed bitterly. 'What makes you so certain
that I value my life? There have been several
moments recently when death would have been
welcome.'

He took the empty coffee-mug from her hand.

'You are hungry and you are starting to talk nonsense. You have everything to live for.'

'A lifetime tied to you? Is that to be my reward for helping to save both our lives from your bloodthirsty colleagues?'

He looked at her consideringly for a long time. 'We could probably have the marriage annulled.'

She did not want to analyse her reaction to this startling piece information. 'On what grounds?' she asked hesitantly.

'That we acted under duress. Or that you practised deliberate deception. I take it that whatever else your your name may be, it isn't Alexandra von Waldstein.'

'No.' She caught her breath on a defiant gasp, not understanding why she felt compelled to goad him. 'My name is Anna Teresa.'

There was a crash as the pieces of pottery mug crashed into the stone fireplace. 'Dammit, woman! Has the time not come to end this farcical pretence? What do you hope to gain by it? Is your anonymity so important to you?'

She was saved the necessity of finding a reply. A young girl tapped on the panels of the door, then entered.

'Your dinner is served, and I am to tell you that Professor Muller has arrived. The meal is in the kitchen and the Professor is waiting for you there.'

CHAPTER
EIGHT

THE first thing Anna noticed about Professor Muller was his distinguished appearance. The second thing she noticed was that he was bone-weary. Despite this evident fatigue, he greeted Stefan with a warm embrace, his tired eyes examining the Prince for signs of his prolonged captivity in the notorious Innesbad prison.

'You look better than I had hoped for, my friend, but then you always did have the constitution of an ox. I heard this morning that you seemed well, when you left the cathedral. It was a great relief to us all.'

Stefan had returned the older man's embrace with enthusiasm. Now he stepped back, cool reserve replacing the previous warmth of his smile.

'Your words remind me that I have apologies to make to you. And I must also present my wife. Herr Professor Muller . . . The Princess Alexandra.'

Anna extended her hand, unconsciously holding it forward in the manner of royalty expecting deference from a commoner. Stefan's eyes flashed a furious message in her direction, but the Professor merely took her hand and bowed over it with impeccable correctness. No observer of the scene could have guessed that he was greeting the woman who had usurped his daughter's rightful position as

Prince Stefan's bride. Anna had wanted to dislike him, but she felt nothing save an instinctive rapport with the man. The man, she reminded herself, who was the leader of the Revolutionary Party, and the man who had written the stirring pamphlets that had inspired the Carthian people to rebellion.

'I understand from my friend Georg that you and Stefan have not eaten today, Princess,' said the Professor. 'Would you care to sit at the table so that we can all eat while Stefan and I discuss some business?'

'I'm very hungry,' she admitted. She looked covertly at the Professor, still trying to reconcile his courtly gentleness with her image of a desperate revolutionary. In fact, none of Stefan's colleagues fitted her preconceived notions of how rebels ought to look and behave. Except perhaps the student, Hans . . .

Stefan escorted her with formal politeness to the wooden kitchen table, and the Professor pulled back her stool with a flourish. The boards were bare, scrubbed clean, and set with pottery bowls and spoons. A large tureen stood in the centre of the table, the only serving dish provided. Not even on childhood picnics had Anna eaten in such primitive surroundings. But then, she thought with a wry inner smile, she had been doing a great many things recently that she had never done before.

The Professor served Anna first, heaping her bowl with a thick vegetable stew. The smell was so tantalising that she could hardly wait until the two men had served themselves before dipping her spoon into the rich broth. She had not realised that such homely food could look so appetising.

Anna ate busily for a few minutes, but she

paused as soon as she noticed that Stefan was observing her closely between taking mouthfuls of his own food.

'Professor,' he said as soon as Anna stopped eating. 'I have to explain to you why I broke my promise to Maria. You know how much I admire and honour your daughter. It distresses me more than I can say, that I have behaved so dishonourably towards her.'

Professor Muller rose from the table and poured some wine into his beaker from a pitcher standing on the kitchen dresser. He sipped at it slowly. 'I imagine you had a good reason for your actions,' he said. For a brief moment his gaze flickered in Anna's direction, and he smiled. 'Other than the obvious ones so many will accuse you of.'

Stefan's gaze did not turn to Anna, even for an instant. 'Franz Johann offered me a bargain,' he said. 'He offered me my life if I married . . . this woman. If I did not agree to the marriage, we would both have been executed.'

'I see.' Professor Muller was silent for a long time, then he reached out to touch Stefan's arm. 'I understand why you did it,' he said.

'Do you?' Hope and bitterness were equally mixed in Stefan's brief response.

'You should have some faith in my powers of intellect, Stefan. After all, I am Professor of Philosophy at Carthia University.' The Professor permitted himself a small smile. 'You are a symbol of hope to the peasants in this duchy; the hope of better times to come. You were afraid that the peasants would take your execution as the signal for an uprising. Carthia is resting on a powder-keg at this moment, and you were afraid that your death would be the match that set alight the explosion.'

A great sigh relaxed Stefan's body and Anna realised just how tense he had been before. 'You do understand,' he said. 'I dared not hope that you would.'

'There are still some mysteries, however,' Professor Muller pointed out. 'Why, Princess, was our new Grand Duke Franz Johann so anxious to see you married to Stefan? What did he hope to gain?'

Anna's bitter laughter expressed all the resentment and frustration that had been building up inside her ever since the death of her parents. 'Ask my *husband*!' she said violently. 'He is so sure he knows the answer to that question!'

Stefan's gaze was as cool and assessing as ever as his eyes raked her flushed features. 'When Franz Johann first insisted upon the match, I thought this woman was a party to his plans. Franz hinted that she was an Austrian, and I assumed she had been instructed first to seduce me and then to spy upon me.'

The Professor's reassuring expression became slightly strained. 'Do you continue to hold that opinion?' he asked.

Stefan was still careful to avoid looking at Anna. 'I have reached no definite conclusion,' he said. 'I know only that she has received the training of a daughter of the aristocracy, although I can't begin to guess how she acquired such training. Her voice and accent alone mark her as a woman who has moved in the highest circles. Trained courtesans, of course, are frequently taught the manners of the nobility.'

Professor Muller turned to Anna. 'Will you not

tell us who you are?' he asked with gentle dignity.
'You must see that you are completely in our power
while you are here. Would it not be easier for you to
tell us truthfully why Franz Johann wanted you to
marry Stefan? Whatever the Grand Duke's original
plans, they have clearly gone awry now you are
with us. It is difficult to see how you can fulfil Franz
Johann's instructions when we are here to monitor
your every move. The plight of the people of
Carthia is a grim one, Princess. Could you not find
the courage to throw your lot in with ours?'

She hardened her heart against the insidious
appeal of his words. She needed to remember that
these men were the enemies of her family and
therefore the enemies of her country. 'I cannot,'
she said and her lips were so stiff it was hard for her
to move them. 'You betrayed my father and helped
cause his death. I can never forget that.'

Professor Muller looked at her with new sympathy. 'So many good people were killed need-
lessly. Who was your father, my dear?'

Anna gave up the pretence of renewed eating,
putting the spoon back in her bowl and staring
down at her hands. She said nothing. She knew she
could not bear to see the Professor's kindly eyes
cloud over with revulsion. She remained silent.

Professor Muller turned to Stefan. 'Has she told
you anything about her family?' he asked.

Stefan sprang to his feet, his stool crashing un-
heeded to the floor as he pushed it violently away
from him. 'I know only that my wife is either a
madwoman or a consummate liar,' he said and fury
kept his words clipped short. 'Tell him who you are,
my dear. You have never hesitated to tell me. And
do not forget, pray, to raise those great eyes of

yours, swimming in tears, so that the Professor may have the full benefit of your pitiful confession.'

Anna's shoulders were shaken by a silent sob and Stefan, seemingly goaded beyond endurance, came and shook her roughly.

'Come, come, my dear! Don't hold back when you have a new audience. Tell us who you are.'

Defiantly, she lifted her head and faced the Professor. 'I am the Princess Anna Teresa of Carthia,' she said. 'My father was the Grand Duke Frederick, until he was murdered by my cousin Franz Johann.'

The pity she had dreaded quickly filled the Professor's face, to be followed by a new reserve. 'I'm sorry that you do not feel able to trust us,' he said. The weariness Anna had seen when she first came into the kitchen returned and flooded his face. He looked at Stefan with a sympathy that was quickly concealed. The Professor, Anna thought with a flash of angry insight, knew better than to offer Stefan open sympathy. 'I think it would be preferable if Stefan and I continued our conversation in private,' the Professor said. 'Have you finished eating, Your Excellency?'

'Yes,' she said, noting regretfully the new formality of his address. 'My appetite doesn't seem to be very large these days.'

'You will feel stronger after a good night's sleep. Georg Schiller is a kind man. He will have found you a comfortable room where you may rest undisturbed.'

'And a reliable revolutionary to guard my door?' Anna queried bitterly. 'Don't worry, Professor, you may count on one certainty. Much as I despise Stefan and his gang of murdering friends, I despise

my cousin more. I will never betray you until Franz
Johann has been brought to justice. Until then you
are safe from me.'

Professor Muller escorted her to the door, but he
paused without opening it. 'My dear, it is obvious
to me that you have been badly hurt and you have
taken refuge in a fairy tale because you are fearful
of trusting the people around you. And why should
you trust us, after all? You do not know us, any
more than we know you. But later, when you have
been with us for a while, you will learn that we are
not murderers and that it is safe to share your
secrets with us.'

He did not seem to expect her to make any reply
and she was glad, for his kindness unnerved her as
no cruelty could ever have done. He pulled open
the door and smiled at Hans, who was guarding the
entrance to the kitchen. Anna wondered if his hint
of constraint towards Hans existed only in her
imagination, or whether it was truly there. 'Prince
Stefan's bride is tired,' the Professor said. 'She
would like to get some sleep. Could you find some
corner of Georg's house where she could be quiet—
and alone?'

'Yes. Georg says she is to have the main bedroom.'

'Excellent. Goodnight, my dear. Life will seem
more cheerful tomorrow morning after a sound
sleep.' He saw her expression and gave a little
laugh. 'Oh yes! I know I speak in platitudes, but
platitudes, you know, often contain a great deal of
good sense. That is why they have been repeated so
frequently.' He patted her arm in a fatherly gesture. At least, Anna supposed it was a fatherly
gesture. The Grand Duke Frederick had not been

much in the habit of giving his children affectionate
hugs and pats.

'Goodnight,' the Professor repeated. He turned
back into the kitchen, shutting the door behind him
so that Anna was left alone in the dark corridor
with Hans. She was aware of a sharp sensation of
loss, and attributed it to the chill of the tiny hallway
after the cosy warmth of the well-lit kitchen.

Hans gave a surly gesture in the direction of the
wooden stairs. 'Your room is up there,' he said.
'Georg's wife and daughter have been forced to
leave the house and stay with their cousin in the
village in order to make room for you and Prince
Stefan. I don't see why you shouldn't sleep in the
barn with the rest of us.'

She ignored his aggressive manner. 'I am most
grateful to Frau Georg Schiller and her daughter,'
she said. 'It has been a very long day for both Prince
Stefan and myself.'

Hans didn't say anything further, even when
they arrived at the bedroom door. He lit the
candle stuck in a pewter stick and it illuminated
a tiny room, furnished with a bed, a metal-hinged
wooden box and nothing else. The polished
wooden floorboards were bare save for two brightly
coloured rugs on either side of the bed. The plump
eiderdown was sheathed in a crisply starched white
cover. The rustic simplicity of the room, which
would have struck Anna as almost barbaric a
couple of weeks previously, now seemed to her to
represent the height of comfort. She sighed with
contentment when she saw there was even some
water in the jug on the washstand.

She turned towards Hans and gave him what she
considered to be a gracious and polite nod of

dismissal. She could not guess how nineteen years of unquestioning obedience from the servants surrounding her affected the quality of her gesture.

'That will be all,' she said. 'Thank Herr Georg for providing so comfortable a room.' She was so anxious to get to bed and find some respite from her problems in sleep that she could almost forget Herr Georg was a rebel who had kidnapped her and was now holding her prisoner. Even when she reminded herself of the truth, the room still looked far more welcoming than the luxurious prison Franz Johann had provided in Innesbad Castle. With an unwelcome flash of insight, she wondered if anybody who opposed Franz Johann's arbitrary methods of government could be *all* bad.

She came out of her reverie and saw that Hans still waited in the doorway. 'I said that would be all,' she repeated.

His eyes flashed with unmistakable hatred. 'What is the use of a revolution that replaces one aristocrat with another?' he asked her. 'It is no accident that Prince Stefan has chosen to marry you, for he is an aristocrat if ever there was one. Poor Maria Muller! She only has virtue and intelligence to recommend her, what competition is that for you?' He stared at her scornfully. 'You!' he spat out. 'With *noblewoman* stamped on every line of your arrogant body!'

There was something faintly ironic in being recognised as a member of the nobility by one of the people who merely despised her for her aristocratic birth. 'How can you be so sure?' Anna asked, curiosity overcoming discretion. 'You told the others that I was an Austrian, sent to spy on you all.'

'You may be Austrian, but you are an aristocrat. I can *smell* aristocrats.' He walked away. 'They all stink of the same corruption,' he said as the door slammed behind him.

Anna wasted a few moments wishing that Stefan's nose could prove as sensitive as Hans's. She shrugged delicately when she realised the futile direction of her thoughts. She bounced up and down on the bed several times, delighted to find it so soft.

The water in the jug was barely tepid when she poured it into the china washbowl, but there was a piece of soap in the dish on the washstand and she was able to remove most of the travel dust that clung to her face and hands. It was only when she ventured to wash the rest of her body that she realised she was faced with an insoluble dilemma. Without the help of a servant, she had no idea how to get undressed. It had taken Franz Johann's maids a quarter of an hour this morning to fasten all the buttons on her wedding-gown. She stretched her fingers awkwardly behind her neck, trying to reach at least some of the tiny, satin-covered buttons. It was no use. She couldn't even reach the top one.

She had no intention of summoning Stefan and informing him of her problem. She was tired of being inspected by his scathing, critical eyes. At least she could remove some of her layers of petticoats. She lifted up the satin skirts of her dress and began the tedious process of untying knots, bows, buttons, hooks, until finally she had shed her horsehair crinoline and all six voluminous petticoats. She piled them in a corner of the room since she had no idea how to set about folding them up, never having performed such a task in her entire life.

She completed her preparations for bed by removing her stockings, which she left on the floor
where they fell, and taking out all the hairpins
which held her hair in place. She had no brush or
comb, so she could only rake her fingers through
the heavy strands, trying to get rid of the worst
tangles.

She was standing in the centre of the tiny room,
wondering if she had sufficient energy to braid her
hair into two plaits for the night, when she heard
the door open. She turned swiftly and was as-
tonished to find Stefan standing in the doorway,
inspecting her through narrowed eyes.

'What is it?' Anna asked. 'Why have you come
in? Why didn't you knock?'

He moved away from the door, bending as he
walked into the room, in order to avoid banging his
head on the low, wooden ceiling. The tiny room
seemed suddenly too small to hold such an over-
powering person. 'It's very late,' he said answering
her question at last. 'I am coming to bed.'

It was several seconds before his meaning penetrated Anna's stupefied mind. 'In *here*? You're
coming to sleep in here? But it's my room!'

'And also mine,' he replied shortly. 'How many
rooms do you suppose Georg has at his disposal?
This is a farmhouse, not a hunting-lodge for the
Austrian aristocracy. It has this bedroom, and a
small storeroom where the Professor is sleeping.
Georg and the other men will spend the night in the
barn.'

'But you can't sleep here. It is not . . . it's not
. . .' Words failed Anna. 'It's immoral,' she concluded lamely.

'Why?' asked Prince Stefan. He had already removed his velvet jacket. He proceeded to untie his cravat, folding it neatly and placing it on the stool next to the washstand. His gaze flickered with a hint of disgust over the untidy mounds of Anna's clothing. He started to unbutton his shirt, and Anna looked hastily away.

'There's only one bed,' she said through tight lips, just as if he might not have noticed the fact.

'I am not an aggressive sleeper. You may have half of it with my goodwill. I have been reliably informed that I don't wriggle.'

'That is not what I meant.' She heard the soft thud as one of his boots fell to the floor and she kept her eyes averted, afraid of what she might see if she turned around. She drew in a deep breath, determined to sound as calm as possible. 'If you sleep here, we cannot get an annulment of our marriage,' she pointed out. She hoped she sounded eminently practical.

'It was never a very good possibility,' he said. His voice sounded weary. 'At the moment, a comfortable bed for tonight seems more important than the doubtful prospect of an annulment a few years from now.'

'I can't sleep with you.' To her chagrin, she felt tears well up in her eyes and overflow on to her cheeks. She heard the soft pad of Stefan's feet on the floor behind her, and felt his hands rest lightly on her shoulders.

'Don't touch me!' she cried. 'How dare you!'

He shrugged. 'I merely intended to unfasten the buttons of your dress so that you could sleep without twenty yards of fabric wrapped around your legs. But that is up to you.'

Common sense warred with years of training, and common sense won. 'I should like to remove my wedding-gown. In fact, I wish I had never put it on,' she declared passionately.

'That would have created a quite unnecessary scandal, I fear. The Archbishop is a liberal-minded fellow, but he is not accustomed to marrying brides clad only in their underclothes.' As so often, she could hear the thread of laughter in his voice and she was warmed by the knowledge that this time he was sharing the laughter with her, not mocking her.

'You know that was not what I meant,' she said answering his smile, and then was furious with herself for succumbing even momentarily to the charm of his address. He has no attractions for me, she told herself sternly. He is the enemy.

'There, I have undone all the buttons. Shall I help you to remove the dress?' His hands lingered for a provocative moment on her bare shoulder.

'No!' She pulled away from his touch, then swivelled away even more hastily when she saw exactly how much of his own clothing he had removed.

'Is that all you are wearing to bed?' she asked in an appalled whisper.

'It is a great deal more than I usually wear.' The hateful laughter was back in his voice, making her heart melt. She forced her face into disapproving lines.

He made no further comment and she watched with secret fascination as he walked to the bed, his naked shoulders displaying a ripple of muscle even in the dim light. 'Wh-what are those marks on your back?' she asked, knowing the answer even before he replied.

'Franz Johann has many ingenious methods of persuading his prisoners to talk. The whipping which gave me those scars was one of his cruder efforts.'

She wanted to touch the ridges of scarred flesh, but of course she could not permit herself such an intimate gesture. She turned aside, closing her eyes to the sight. When she looked round, Stefan was already in the bed.

'Blow out the candle before you come into bed, will you, please? We don't want to burn down Georg's house.' He yawned lazily, then stretched out on one side of the bed, pulling the eiderdown over his half-naked body.

'Are you not tired?' he asked. 'Are you not anxious to come to bed now that I have played lady's-maid so that you can be comfortable?'

She blushed at the possible implications of his words and stood irresolutely in the centre of the room, clutching her wedding-gown in front of her, although she was completely covered by her chemise.

'You might make ad-advances upon my person,' Anna said stiltedly, stumbling with embarrassment as she gave voice to fears that she really knew must be groundless. Stefan, after all, did not even like her.

His laughter was curt, no longer friendly. 'My dear *wife*, you flatter yourself.' He turned away, clearly no longer interested in whether she came to bed or not. She heard him smother another yawn. She was quite sure his eyes, if she could have seen them, would be closed.

She blew out the candle and crept up to the bed, placing herself gingerly on the edge farthest away from Stefan. She lay stiffly in the darkness listening to the steady rhythm of his breathing. Could he possibly have fallen asleep already? Was she so unattractive that he didn't care to stay awake long enough to find out whether or not she had joined him in the bed? For all he knew, she might be sleeping on the bare floor.

She turned her face into the pillow and sobbed quietly for several minutes without quite knowing why. It eventually occurred to her that there was something terribly wrong with crying because a villainous rebel had not wanted to make love to her. The realisation of where her thoughts were leading was so devastating that her mind refused to cope with the implications and she finally fell asleep, too tired to struggle with so many threatening new ideas.

As soon as he felt her body relax, Stefan turned over and stared down at her, his eyes narrowing. His body was taut as a bowstring and he wondered wryly if his wife—he shied away from the word—if the woman in his bed could possibly have been deceived by the pretence of indifference he had struggled to maintain. Could she be as innocent as she seemed? No, of course not. He answered his own silent question. She had clutched her wedding-gown in front of her with a charming pretence of modesty but, with the skill of a trained courtesan, she had placed her body directly in front of the candle so that her slender figure was perfectly outlined by the flickering flame. She must have guessed how her perfume intoxicated him every time he came near her. She must have known how badly he longed to throw caution to the four winds and make love to her until they both finally fell asleep, sated with passion.

The delicate sweep of her lashes curled against cheeks that seemed soft, even childlike, as she relaxed in sleep. He had to resist an overwhelming desire to lean over and kiss the smoothness of her cheek. He flung himself back on his own side of the bed, staring through the darkness at the wooden ceiling. God! He hadn't survived two months of hell in Franz Johann's dungeons, only to succumb to a woman. This was obviously a trap that had been carefully set by his brother, who was no doubt hoping that the weeks of solitary confinement would make the woman seem doubly desirable.

Stefan forced himself to think about her objectively. She was beautiful, of course, with an incredible air of vulnerability which merely served to heighten her charm. She had the capacity, invaluable in a female spy, of appearing innocent in the most unlikely circumstances. She was a convincing actress and he had to keep reminding himself that she had not been betrayed. The quivering mouth, so warm and inviting, had probably kissed more men than she could remember. The hints of fragility were all a pretence.

He pushed the memory of her tear-sparkled eyes angrily aside. Genuine grief caused blotched faces and red-rimmed eyelids, not violet pools of tender misery. The freedom of Carthia hung in the balance and he was allowing himself to be manipulated by a skilfully-trained Austrian whore. He thumped the feather pillow and turned over so that he couldn't see the woman lying so . ... trustingly . . . by his side. Stefan swore long and fluently beneath his breath. God knew, he had problems enough ahead of him without allowing his common sense to be drugged by the slender body of this woman who happened to be his wife.

Perhaps he would leave her behind . . . He had no obligations to her . . . Tomorrow he would tell the Professor that he would go alone to recover the documents . . . Leave her, whatever her real name was, with Georg . . . Georg was a good man, he would take care of her. It would be terrible if she came to any harm . . . Hell and damnation! What did it matter whether she was well-cared for or not? The weariness caused by weeks of deprivation finally caught up with him, and Stefan drifted into a light sleep.

Anna wasn't sure what sound it was that alerted her. For the past week she had been in the habit of sleeping with one ear constantly primed for a hint of danger. She opened her eyes and saw the thin figure of the student, Hans, bending over her husband. Before she could force her vocal chords into a scream, Stefan had sprung out of bed and whirled around so that his assailant was trapped beneath him.

'What were you trying to do?' Stefan asked.

Hans wriggled impotently on the bed and Anna spotted the thin gleam of steel. 'Oh dear heaven! He has a knife!'

Stefan's hand whipped out and in an instant he had recovered the hunting knife from the folds of the eiderdown. 'Talk, Hans, I need an explanation very quickly.'

'You don't understand,' Hans said sullenly. 'I've been sent to warn you. The others have gone already. I was on early morning lookout and a messenger came to say that soldiers are headed this way: they looked like soldiers of the Grand Duke's personal bodyguard. The officers were wearing yellow-and-blue silk sashes, so the messenger said.'

'I see.' Stefan relaxed his hold on Han's body, but he still didn't permit him to get off the bed. 'Why all the secrecy? Why did you need a knife?'

'I wanted to tell you before we woke your wife. I didn't want her to be frightened,' Hans said. 'And the knife fell out of my belt, that's all.' The student was resentful of the interrogation, and he did not bother to conceal the fact.

Stefan moved away from Hans, handing him back the knife. He started to pull on some clothes he removed from the box in the corner of the room.

'Where's Georg gone? I must ask him if he can find somewhere to hide my wife. I'm sure he knows some safe spot in the locality.' Just for a moment, Stefan's gaze flickered towards Anna. 'I'll send for you once it's safe,' he said abruptly before turning back to face Hans. 'Has the Professor left also? I ought to confer with him again before I leave. He should have woken me.'

It seemed to Anna that Hans shifted uneasily as Stefan spoke, but he answered readily enough. 'The Professor had no time to confer with you. You don't seem to realise how close those soldiers are! Georg has gone to fetch his wife and daughters from the village, so that he can show the soldiers everything is just as it always is. You must leave, Prince Stefan. You must leave right away. I will take care of your wife.'

Stefan was fastening the buckle of his belt, and his fingers faltered for an instant. 'Where will you take her?' he asked, not looking at Anna.

'Naturally I will take the greatest care of her. It

will be easy for me to hide her. I know every inch of this area because I was born less than ten miles from here.'

'No!' Anna sprang out of bed, compelled by an urgency she didn't understand. 'I won't stay with him,' she declared.

Stefan pulled on his boots. 'You have no choice.'

Anna's brittle defiance wavered and collapsed into panic. After so many betrayals, she felt safer with Stefan who openly professed his scorn, than she did with somebody who offered her easy friendship. Besides, some instinct made her flesh creep when Hans came close to her. It was the same sensation she had felt whenever Franz Johann touched her, and this time she planned to trust her basic instincts. Her eyes filled with tears and she brushed them aside impatiently. She couldn't remember any other period of time when she had cried so frequently. She knelt down close to Stefan, seizing his hands in an unconscious gesture of frantic appeal.

'Please,' she said, 'don't leave me, Stefan.' She gulped, despising herself for her weakness, but unable to deny how badly she needed him. 'I feel . . . safe . . . with you,' she murmured and her embarrassment caused her voice to catch on a husky note of appeal.

There was silence for several tense seconds, then Stefan pulled his hands out of her grasp. 'It would be dangerous for you to come with me. Hans will keep you safe.'

'Of course,' Hans said smoothly.

'I won't go with him.'

'I don't have time to argue with you,' Stefan said grimly. 'You are endangering us all with these childish arguments.' He tied the wristbands of the gathered sleeves of a typical Carthian peasant shirt. He stuck a hunting-knife in the thick leather belt at his waist, then bundled up the discarded clothes he had worn for their wedding. He handed them to Hans.

'Burn them, will you? By the way, I'm sorry I sprang at you like that just now. You should have known better than to creep up on an old soldier. You might have been killed.'

'It's all right. I understand.' Hans took the bundle of clothes. Stefan was already searching the tiny room for traces of their occupancy and Hans helped him.

'Get dressed, please,' Stefan said to Anna. 'You will have to wear your wedding clothes again. Hans will find you something more practical once he has taken you to safety. There's no time to burn so many yards of fabric and nowhere to hide it, either. Come, quickly, let me help you dress. Minutes are precious.'

'No,' she said defiantly. She saw a flash of emotion in his face and suspected it was anger. She tried to explain her irrational refusal to leave him. 'Please don't make me stay with Hans. *You* are my husband. There is something about . . .' She broke off uncomfortably. How could she say that she didn't trust Hans, when the student was standing only a few feet away from her, looking at her intently?

For a moment, Stefan's gaze rested on her thoughtfully, then he walked impatiently to the bed and shook up the pillows to make sure no loose buttons or jewelled hairpins remained in the covers.

'I have already explained to you that I must travel swiftly and alone. Please get dressed without further discussion. I have warned you that you are endangering us all.'

'I won't go. Unless you permit me to come with you, I won't get dressed.'

'Then remain half-naked, Madam. It is of no great moment to me whether you carry your clothes or wear them.'

'I will neither wear them nor carry them,' she said. 'So what will you do with all my clothes? There is no time to bury them. There's no time to burn them, you said so yourself. Hans may be strong enough to drag me to some hiding-place against my will, but how is he going to carry all my clothes at the same time? You will have to leave them here. They will be positive proof to the soldiers that we have been in Herr Georg's house.' With a ruthlessness that was foreign to her true nature, she added, 'Georg and his family will die.'

Stefan was white with fury, although Anna was sure she glimpsed some other emotion in his eyes. 'Why you scheming vixen . . .' He grabbed one of her petticoats and tried to pull it over her head, but she let her body go limp and he could not struggle with the folds of material at the same time as he held her upright. He swore violently, finally thrusting the garments into her hands.

'You have ten minutes to clothe yourself, Madam. And don't think you have won a great victory. I don't know what your game is, but you'll regret insisting on coming with me. Hurry, Hans. Let's burn my clothes while she dresses herself.' He stormed out of the room, slamming the sturdy wooden door behind him.

Anna did not give herself any time to think about what had happened. She pulled on her layers of petticoats with feverish haste, scrambling to tie the laces and ribbons. She was filled with dread in case Stefan left without her, and she was panting with exertion when she finally pulled the wedding-gown over her head. Stefan walked into the room just as she thrust her arms into the sleeves of her dress.

'You dressed quickly,' he said. 'What is to stop me refusing to take you now you are dressed?'

She went whiter than her dress. 'You . . . wouldn't . . .'

There was a slight pause. 'No,' he said. 'But do not try to cross swords with me, madam. You will be the loser. Why haven't you put on your crinoline?' He gestured to the padded cage that had supported her voluminous skirts.

'It's too heavy. I'll carry it until we find somewhere to dispose of it.'

He looked for a moment as though he would argue, then he turned on his heel and indicated that she should follow him. 'Hans has the horses waiting for us,' he said. 'Hurry, for you have put all our lives at risk with your obstinacy.'

She followed him down the stairs, her dress almost falling off her shoulders because she had not managed to fasten a single one of the tiny satin buttons. She clutched her layers of skirt in one hand and clung to the crinoline with the other. She wondered what fiend had first decreed that ladies of fashion should encase themselves in so many yards of useless silk and satin.

Hans waited in a small courtyard, holding two

horses. There was no sign of another living soul. From the barn in the distance she heard the soft lowing sound of the animals, eager to be turned loose and led to their spring pasture. It seemed a typical farm scene such as she remembered from childhood visits with her governess. It was hard to believe so much intrigue and potential violence simmered beneath the peaceful surface.

Stefan's impatient voice cut into her thoughts. 'Mount, please.'

The smaller of the two horses stood alongside an upturned wooden trough that Hans evidently thought she could use as a mounting block. As she climbed on to the trough, she realised the horse was saddled with nothing more than a thick woven pad, buckled to the leather girth. 'I need a side-saddle,' she said, knowing even as she spoke that Stefan could not possibly provide her with any such luxury.

'If you cannot cope with your horse, madam, you have the choice of remaining with Hans. I cannot delay while you complain. It is forty minutes since we learned that soldiers have been sighted. They are probably not more than three or four miles from here.'

'Less,' said Hans. 'If this farm had not been in the valley, they would be able to spot us by now.'

Anna gritted her teeth, determined not to let Stefan defeat her. It had become a personal battle of wills between them now and pride would not let her admit his victory.

'Hold the horse still,' she ordered Hans and mounted the animal, feeling her skirts bunch up all around her thighs. It was vastly improper, agonisingly uncomfortable and not at all safe. Nevertheless, she was on the horse. She stared rebelliously at Stefan.

'I am ready to leave,' she said.

'You have forgotten your crinoline,' he remarked. 'It has fallen off the mounting block.'

She spoke to Hans through tightly clenched teeth. 'Would you be good enough to hand me the crinoline?'

He started to comply with her request, when Stefan intervened. 'Tie it behind me,' he said. He offered no explanation of his order. He pointed with his riding-crop to the open gate of the farmyard.

'Are you ready to gallop, Madam?'

She wouldn't admit to him that her stomach was already heaving with terror as the horse pawed the ground restlessly. She was a superb rider under normal conditions. Riding in a wedding-gown, supported only by a blanket, was outside her range of experience.

'I am waiting to leave,' she replied coolly.

'Stand back from the horses,' Stefan ordered Hans.

'You haven't told me where you're going,' he said quickly. 'What shall I tell the Professor when I meet up with him?'

Stefan looked into the distance for just a minute. 'Tell him we are travelling to the north,' he said. 'I will go to the rendezvous the Professor organised last January. He will remember it is a house on the border, near Bavaria.'

'Close to your main estate?' Hans asked.

'Yes,' Stefan answered slowly. 'The Professor will know where I mean.' Without looking round, he faced his horse towards the gate. 'Are you coming, madam? I shall not wait for you.'

Staring straight ahead of her, trying not to listen to the fearful pounding of her heart, Anna rode out of the courtyard behind her husband.

CHAPTER
NINE

HE broke into a slow canter soon after they left the farm, but for some reason he did not urge his horse into the gallop he had threatened. Anna was in the dangerous position of controlling her mount by pressure on the bit alone, since her skirts wadded in such a way that her body could offer no guidance to the horse whatsoever. It would have been dangerous to gallop, she would almost certainly have been thrown. She wondered why Stefan, who must have known this, kept the horses to a canter. It would have been such an easy way to rid himself of a problem wife. It was a few minutes before it occurred to her that a dead woman dressed in tattered wedding clothes would soon be found by the soldiers and would give them a sure clue as to the direction Stefan had taken in his escape. She had no idea why this piece of sensible reasoning left her feeling so depressed.

The task of staying on her horse was too difficult to allow Anna much time for observing the passing scene, and they were at the edge of some woods before she realised just where their journey was taking them. She shivered. The memories of her last flight into the forest were still far too fresh to be comfortable. She was so busy trying to keep herself calm that she almost ran into Stefan's horse before she saw that he had pulled his animal to a halt.

'What is it?' she asked.

Stefan dismounted quickly, tying his horse to a small tree-trunk. 'Get down,' he said. 'I will hold your horse while you dismount.'

The fear she had tried to control filled her, making her mouth dry and knotting her stomach with a sharp pain. Had he decided they were now far enough from the farm for him to dispose of her body? 'I will k-keep up, Stefan. I w-will not trouble you.' Pride prevented her begging more explicitly for her life. She had humbled herself in front of Franz Johann, but she wouldn't humble herself before this man.

He looked at her strangely. 'What do you imagine I intend to do? I merely plan to bury some of your clothes.'

'Oh.' She was shaken by a surge of overwhelming relief and for a moment her body slumped in reaction. She quickly straightened her shoulders once again, and swung her leg carefully over the horse's back. Dismounting was not an easy task, even though Stefan spoke soothingly to the horse so that it remained virtually motionless.

Her legs were shaking when she stood on the bumpy forest path. Stefan tethered her horse next to his own, then removed a short-handled axe from his saddle-bags. He started to hack out a rectangular hollow, peeling the turf back carefully.

'We should burn everything,' he said. 'But there simply isn't time and the smoke would alert everybody for miles around to our presence. If the soldiers look carefully, they'll find this pit. Let's hope they don't look carefully. Give me that damn crinoline, and start talking off your clothes.'

She walked over to his horse and untied the

crinoline from behind his saddle. She removed all her petticoats at the same time, standing behind a concealing bush. Her feet, clad only in satin shoes, were already aching abominably from the pressure of iron stirrups against her soles, but she said nothing at all, trying to disguise her limp as she walked back to him. Nothing on earth would persuade her to give Stefan an excuse to leave her behind.

She saw that he had dug out a fair-sized pit. He took the clothing from her, spreading it all over the hollow and trampling it as far into the soft soil as it would go. He poured water from his drinking canteen over one of the petticoats, and indicated to Anna that she should fetch water from the nearby stream to wet all the clothes. They certainly lay more compactly once they were wet.

It required many trips to the stream before the clothes were sufficiently sodden to satisfy Stefan. He straightened at last, walked to the stream and stripped off his jacket and shirt, splashing water all over his head and body.

'The water seems clear enough,' he said to Anna. 'You'd better drink here. Who knows where we'll next find water.' He stood on the bank of the stream shaking himself dry before pulling on his shirt. 'You haven't taken off your wedding-dress,' he said. 'You can't keep that on. It's not safe to ride in.'

'I have no other clothes,' she reminded him shortly.

He immediately strode over to his horse and unpacked a crumpled white shirt and a pair of trousers from the saddle bags. 'You'd better take these,' he said, holding them out to her. 'I can't spend the rest of the day trotting along the roads as if I were out for an afternoon ride in the country air. You must be dressed in such a way that you can gallop.'

Two weeks earlier, Anna reflected, she would probably have fainted at the idea of putting on a pair of man's breeches. Even two days earlier she would have blushed and protested. But when Stefan thrust the worn shirt and battered trousers into her hands, all she felt was relief and a faint stirring of gratitude. Whatever Stefan pretended, she was quite sure this early halt so close to the edge of the forest had been made because he worried about her comfort and safety. She took the breeches with a shy smile. 'Thank you, Stefan. I will change very quickly. Wearing these clothes, I'll be able to keep up with you easily. My father liked a woman who could keep up with the hunt, so I have been trained to ride fast. When I was a child, I was even allowed to ride using a boy's saddle.'

Stefan smiled as she started speaking, then he turned away abruptly, his face shuttered. 'Hurry up and remove your wedding-dress, madam. I will bury it while you put on the breeches and shirt.'

She dressed behind the leafy bush and was ready before Stefan had finished replacing the turf. She led her horse to the stump of a fallen oak tree and used it as a mounting-block. She watched Stefan stamp on the sod as he replaced each rough rectangle, and finally he dragged a few fallen branches to cover the raw incision marks made by the axe. He didn't pause to admire his handiwork, but mounted his horse quickly and together they cantered out of the forest.

Anna knew better than to question him as to

where they were going. In any case, once they were free of the forest she had no breath left for asking questions. Stefan pointed his horse away from the main highway and led them into the foothills where they were forced to go in single file along the narrow track. He set the pace at a slow gallop and Anna's considerable riding skill was strained to its limits. She was grateful for her kid gloves. They were the only item from her wedding wardrobe that had the least practicality, she thought wryly. Without them, the palms of her hands would have been as blistered as the soles of her feet.

After almost three hours of hard riding her animal was beginning to shudder beneath her and she was relieved when Stefan checked his mount and their pace slackened to a fast walk. She hadn't tried to identify the direction in which they were riding, but as they slowed down she realised that the sun was positioned behind them and they were, in fact, heading-south-west. The forest had been to the north of Georg's farm but, since burying her clothes, Stefan had led them steadily away from the direction he had told Hans they would be taking.

The terrain was becoming increasingly rocky underfoot and increasingly mountainous on the horizon. When their path was crossed by a shallow stream, Stefan pulled his horse to a halt and vaulted lightly out of the saddle. Wearily, almost too tired to be grateful for the halt, Anna dismounted. She sank on to a patch of grass, retaining just enough energy to keep a tight hold on the reins of her horse. Her feet were two blazing lumps of pain. Despite the soft leather of the breeches, her thighs were rubbed raw. She spoke quickly to Stefan, so that she wouldn't have time to think about her pain.

'Why aren't we riding north?'

'Because my rendezvous with Professor Muller lies south.'

'Why did you lie to Hans?'

Stefan gathered a bunch of long grasses, wrapped them around his hand and began to wipe down the horses. 'I have learned that it is safer not to trust anybody more than is absolutely necessary.'

'It seems a wise decision. Especially somebody you have found standing over you with a knife.'

He looked at her then. 'I wondered if you believed our friend's glib explanations.'

'I have learned to be as wary as you,' she said. 'And yet you were prepared to leave me in Hans's care. You told me he would protect me. With his knife, perhaps?'

Stefan continued to rub the horses. 'I never intended to leave you behind,' he said quietly. 'Hans would have been suspicious if I had seemed too anxious to take you with me.'

She wished she could believe him. She wanted so badly to trust somebody again. But how could she hope to build a trusting relationship with a man who would not even believe her true identity? She started to speak, then fell silent. The truth, she had learned, was not always the invaluable weapon her governess had taught her. Any mention of her parents always brought on an explosion of icy wrath from Stefan, and she did not want to disrupt the precarious truce they had managed to establish during the past few hours.

'Where are we going?' she asked in the end. It seemed a neutral enough question.

'I am planning to cross into the Italian peninsula. We are going to a small, northern Italian village.'

'Why are you running the risk of remaining in the Austrian Empire when you could escape into Germany?'

'Why should you care if I run the risk of capture? If I am dead, you are free.'

'If you die, I am very likely to die with you,' Anna said quietly. 'Besides, I do not wish to see you dead, even though I can't support your cause.'

'And what cause do you support, my dear wife?' Stefan asked curtly and Anna realised that despite all her careful forethought, her questions had disturbed their few, fleeting moments of harmony.

'I don't know,' she said uncertainly, determined to answer him with honesty. 'I have always been taught that the hereditary principle of government ensures stability and justice for the people. But when I see Franz Johann . . .' She broke off, appalled at what she had admitted. She hadn't even realised she harboured such thoughts. She certainly wasn't prepared to share them with Stefan, a revolutionary and the avowed enemy of her family. 'I'm hungry,' she said stiffly, not looking at him. 'How much longer is it before we rendezvous with Professor Muller?'

'I estimate two days. If we are lucky we should reach a safe house before nightfall tomorrow.'

'Two days!' The horror she felt forced the words out in a high-pitched squeak.

'Do you have any objections to accompanying me? I can leave you behind if you prefer it. You are a safe distance from my revolutionary colleagues, if you genuinely believe they are a threat to you.' He shrugged, not bothering to watch her reaction as he guided his horse to the stream. 'Follow that tiny track to the left and you will find a village not more than two miles due west of here. Turn yourself in to the local military garrison. They will be happy to escort you back to Franz Johann's protection.'

'What are you hoping for?' she asked bitterly. 'That the garrison will rape me, or that Franz Johann will murder me and thus relieve you of a tiresome encumbrance?'

'Neither.' Stefan was busy adjusting the girth on his horse's saddle and it was impossible to see his face. 'I take it you prefer to travel with me?'

'Prefer is not an appropriate word. I *must* travel with you if I wish to live.'

'Am I to conclude that you trust me more than you trust Franz Johann's men? My dear wife, I am flattered.'

'I trust you not to murder me. Besides, I trust almost anybody more than I trust cousin Franz.'

His face froze into an expression of controlled fury, and too late she realised what she had said. 'Stefan,' she said urgently, springing up and reaching out to touch him. 'I didn't mean to refer to him as my cousin. It just slipped out . . .'

He pulled his arm away, turning his back on her pleading expression. 'Go and drink some water from the stream,' he said. 'Then remount. We have a lot of rough ground to cover if we are to reach a safe resting place before nightfall.'

She went obediently to the stream and splashed her face with the cold water. It tasted fresh and bubbling and helped her to forget the emptiness of her stomach. She didn't dare to enquire if Stefan's saddle-bags contained any food. She heard his voice behind her, uttering a string of profanities and she turned round in surprise. Surely she hadn't done anything new to provoke his anger?

'What is it?' she asked. 'What have I done?'

'Your feet,' he replied curtly. 'There is blood all over your shoes. You obstinate fool, why didn't you say anything to me?'

She looked at him steadily. 'I did not wish to give you an excuse for leaving me behind. And I cannot see how you can cure the problem. Even you cannot turn satin wedding-slippers into leather riding-boots.'

'Sit down,' he said brusquely, ignoring her attempt at defiance. He pulled off his leather jacket and removed his shirt, slashing at the ends of it with the knife he wore stuck in his belt. He soaked one strip in the spring water.

'Remove your shoes and stockings.'

'I cannot.'

'Why ever not?'

She blushed and looked away, not wanting to confess that she dreaded the thought of his strong fingers touching any part of her body. 'I would have to roll up my . . . breeches.'

He looked at her blankly for a moment, then laughed with unflattering scorn. 'My dear wife, this attack of maidenly modesty is unnecessary. I assure you that I am currently too preoccupied with minor matters—such as the imminent likelihood of my capture and death—to be overcome by uncontrollable lust at the mere sight of your naked ankle, or even your knee. Delectable though such sights may normally be, you are safe with me, madam. Take your shoes and stockings off, or I shall perform the task for you.'

She blushed more deeply than before, feeling as foolish as it was possible to feel. She wished she could remind him that she was a princess and not accustomed to stripping off portions of her clothing in public view. Her mouth twisted wryly at the thought of his reaction if she attempted any such explanation. She tugged at her stockings, wincing when she removed her torn shoes. Blood from her blistered feet had stuck stockings, shoes and skin together in a tight, painful bond.

'I will do the rest,' Stefan said, brushing her hand away. His manner was cold, almost angry, but his fingers seemed gentle as they eased her blistered feet away from the tattered stockings. Deftly, he bathed the swollen skin with cool spring water, wrapping thin dry strips from his shirt in a bandage that covered the worst of her blisters.

'If you had pointed out how inadequate your shoes were,' he said when the bandages were in place, 'I could have saved some strips from your petticoats and made a more adequate form of protection.'

She said nothing. Fear of admitting to any weakness had kept her silent, but she was not prepared to tell him yet again how frightened she was at the thought of being separated from him. He observed her silently, then made several quick, angry nicks in her satin shoes. 'Put these and your stockings on again. I have cut them so that they will fit over the bandages. They are likely to be of some use in protecting you from the stirrups, I suppose.'

'Thank you.' She finished tying the satin ribbons and looked up, forcing herself to meet his eyes. 'I appreciate your consideration, Stefan.'

'It's time to mount. We have wasted more than enough time already.'

When she was once more in the saddle, he rummaged in his pack and returned with a piece of hard cheese and a thick slice of wheat bread. 'Here,' he said. 'Eat that before we set off. It was all Hans and I could find in the rush.'

'Thank you.'

'I don't want you fainting, that's all.'

'I won't faint.'

There was reluctant admiration in his face when he looked at her at last. 'No,' he said. 'I don't expect you will.'

She kept her promise, but only just. She was light-headed when he finally reined in his horse and fell back beside her.

'Do you see the lights up ahead?' He indicated with his crop and she nodded, forgetting that he couldn't see her clearly in the darkness. He must have sensed her reply, for he continued speaking softly.

'I am going to check that it's safe for us to approach. You stay here.'

She was afraid of being alone in the shadowy darkness. 'I would prefer to come with you,' she said and her voice sounded haughty because she was so scared.

'You will be safe here, I promise.' He seemed to understand the cause of her gruffness and for a moment she felt his hand resting lightly on her shoulders. 'I checked carefully as we rode up, and there are no soldiers within a radius of ten miles, I'll swear it. If you keep the horses quiet, nobody will know you are here.'

'What about you? What is it down there? Is it another one of your rebel hideouts?'

He did not reply for a moment. 'It's an inn,' he said eventually. 'Just a simple country inn. We have covered over fifty miles today and we are close to the Brenner pass. It's better if we wait until daylight before we make our crossing into Italy.'

She wondered if he had guessed that she was at the point of exhaustion. Certainly *he* seemed in no need of a rest. 'Won't the soldiers have a better chance of finding us if we wait until daybreak?'

She saw the white flash of his teeth as he smiled in the darkness. 'I doubt if Franz Johann's soldiers have travelled this far south. Anyway, they will be looking for a prince and his bride. Somehow, I don't think we shall be recognised.'

She heard laughter in his voice and looked down at her stained leather breeches, held up around her waist with a length of rope and topped by a dusty, crumpled shirt. 'Perhaps you are right,' she said sharing his silent laughter despite her tiredness.

He turned to face her, and she could see he was still smiling. 'We just need some sort of cap to cover your hair. Those chestnut curls would betray you as a woman anywhere.'

'I can cut them,' she said recklessly. 'Crop them close to my head.'

He turned away, his smile fading. 'I should prefer to find you a cap,' he said. He jumped down from his horse without saying anything further and put the reins into her hands. He pulled the leather jacket tight, so that it concealed the whiteness of his shirt. He moved so softly along the path that Anna could scarcely keep track of his movements. She peered into the blackness, watching intently until he faded into the shadows of the trees. She would not admit to herself that she was afraid—not for herself, but for Stefan.

It seemed hours before he returned. 'It's safe,' he

said briefly. 'I've made arrangements with the inn-keeper so that we can go straight to the bedroom. I will lead your horse down the path. It's very narrow.'

The inn yard was deserted and without lights as he led the horses into a wooden shed that would serve as their stable for the night. He tethered the animals, hanging their saddles on wooden hooks stuck into the primitive walls. 'I'll take care of the animals if you'll sit down,' he said quietly.

'I can do my share,' she protested, although her legs were practically collapsing beneath her.

'Don't argue.' Stefan's movements were as brisk as his commands. Anna wondered if he ever felt normal human fatigue. Twelve hours in the saddle, and he scarcely looked exercised. She had to admit that it was heaven to stretch out her aching limbs on a pile of hay . . . She was asleep as soon as she sat down.

'Time to go.' Stefan's voice sounded gently in her ear. She stirred, still half-asleep It was pleasant when Sefan spoke to her so softly, his mouth curved into a smile. She felt his arms around her, lifting her from the straw, and she knew she ought to resist the delight that flooded through her. Instead, she welcomed the comfort offered by his strength. She lifted her head and found herself staring into the depths of his cold grey eyes. Except at this moment they weren't cold at all. They flamed with a warmth that threatened to envelop her, burning away all memory of the old Princess Anna Teresa and leaving only a woman, Stefan's wife. She blinked, returning rapidly to full consciousness.

'Put me down!' she said, panic making her voice sound sharp.

'Of course.'

'I . . . er . . . I fell asleep,' she said unnecessarily as they walked across the cobbled yard.

'So I see.' Stefan's expression was unreadable in the darkness of the night. He reached up, as if to touch her face, and Anna jumped. 'There's straw in your hair,' he said prosaically.

'Oh!' She wanted to change the subject, so she asked the first question that came into her head. 'Where are all the guests?'

They had almost reached the door of the inn, but Anna could hear no sounds of customers drinking and laughing inside. 'This isn't a local gathering-place,' Stefan said. 'This is a smuggling route; it has been for years. The innkeeper is a man who's willing to keep his mouth shut about everything if you pay him enough. He's learned never to ask unnecessary questions, and he's learned the value of honesty. Our horses are safe here, which is more than they would be in most country inns.'

Anna's body was shaken by a wrenching burst of hysterical laughter. It was all too ridiculous. Two weeks ago she had been entertaining the members of the Court to an elegant betrothal ball, the most urgent problem on her mind being whether to wear her blue silk or her pale yellow taffeta dress. Tonight she was standing at the door of a smuggler's den, and worrying whether she had fallen in love with the leader of the revolutionaries. As she realised what she had thought, her laughter changed suddenly to tears, which cascaded down her cheeks in a seemingly endless stream.

Stefan pushed up the heavy wooden latch and shoved her unceremoniously inside the door.

'You're tired,' he said curtly. 'Our room is through here.'

He guided her quickly out of the brightly-lit passageway into a tiny cubicle of a room. It was already lit by a smoky oil-lamp and contained absolutely nothing in the way of furniture save a bed covered by a straw mattress and a single knitted blanket. She knew the mattress was stuffed with straw, because wisps of it hung out of a split in the mattress cover. Stefan deposited the saddle bags next to the bed.

She sank wearily on to the bed, putting away all thoughts of a steaming bath and fresh clothes. There were no pillows, but she was too tired to care. She wondered if there were lice or fleas in the bed, then wished she hadn't thought of such a possibility.

'Wait here,' Stefan said. 'There is a bolt on the door. Use it, and don't open the door to anyone save me.'

She was too dispirited to protest at his dictatorial tone. She barred the door as he instructed and had drifted into a state of semi-stupor when she heard a short, sharp tap on the door.

'Stefan?'

'Yes.'

He came in quickly when she unbarred the door. He was carrying a bucket of steaming hot water and a bundle of clothing, wrapped in a white shirt.

'Here.' He held the clothes out to her. 'The innkeeper has a son, and I bought these from him. They will fit you better than that makeshift outfit of mine.'

'Thank you.' She was grateful for his thoughtful gesture. Although he rarely spoke to her kindly,

Anna realised that she had received more true consideration from him in the past two days than she had ever received from the members of her family. Her eyes misted with fresh tears, and she dashed them away angrily. She wasn't going to cry in front of him *again*.

'What's the matter now?' She recognised the exasperation in his voice and she turned away to hide the traces of tears.

'I'm tired, that's all. The water . . . is it for me?'

'Yes. There's a towel inside that bundle. I'm afraid the innkeeper didn't have any soap. It doesn't seem to be a commodity he finds much use for.'

'The hot water will be fine.'

'I am going to see about some food for our supper. We'll eat it in here.' He walked out of the room, leaving Anna free to strip off her filthy clothes and make the best use she could of the hot water in the bucket. It was truly amazing, she concluded, how ingenious one could become over the details of getting oneself clean without a bath or soap or a washcloth.

She was already washed and dressed in clean underclothes, covered by the boy's shirt, when Stefan came back into their room. He looked for a moment at her long, bare legs and Anna felt a strange warmth curl through her toes and spread throughout her body. Stefan turned away abruptly and carried the tray he was holding over to the bed. Two big wooden bowls, two wooden spoons and two tin mugs, reposed on the tray. Anna inspected the bounty with ravenous eyes.

'The innkeeper's kitchen is cleaner than the rest

of his property,' Stefan remarked. 'But I took the precaution of re-washing all the utensils.'

'It looks delicious.' Anna was already sipping the contents of her mug. 'What's this?'

Stefan looked at her strangely. 'Beer,' he said shortly.

Anna drank again. 'It's bitter,' she said. 'But good. I have never tasted beer before.'

Stefan made no reply, but she was too hungry to care. Surely he couldn't object to the fact that she'd never tasted beer? She ate every mouthful of the stew before putting her spoon down with a sigh of pleasure. She swallowed the last few sips of beer and had difficulty smothering her yawns. The bed was even narrower than the one they had slept in the night before, but she was tired enough to have fallen asleep on the floor.

'Are you coming to bed now?' she asked Stefan.

His features seemed to tighten. 'No,' he said. He carried the tray away from the bed where they had been eating and put it on the floor inside the door. 'How are your feet?' he asked.

'Sore,' she grimaced, but did not elaborate on the swollen mess hidden beneath the clean socks Stefan had provided.

'I'll find you some leather shoes before tomorrow morning,' he said. He picked up the bucket of water she had used for washing and set it down next to the tray. 'I must take these back to the kitchen, or we'll have ra . . . mice scurrying around the room.' He hesitated on the threshold as if debating within himself, then turned and spoke to her quickly.

'Do you want me to comb your hair for you? It looks . . . tangled.'

'I don't have a comb, or a brush.'

'I do.' He searched for a moment or two in one of the saddlebags and produced a tortoiseshell comb. 'If you will sit on the bed, I'll try to untangle the snarls without hurting you.'

She sat obediently on the edge of the bed. She was well-used to the nightly ritual of having somebody brush her hair. A maid had performed the task every night of her life until the day her parents died. She shook the heavy mass over her shoulders and felt Stefan's hands resting against the nape of her neck. She shuddered, without understanding why.

She was aware of an intolerable tension building between them as his strong fingers untwisted the tangled curls. Neither of them spoke until he laid aside the comb and said in a husky voice. 'I've finished.'

She turned to thank him, but the words died away on her lips. She saw that his eyes blazed with some emotion she had never seen before, and she felt heat flame in her cheeks. His gaze became fixed on her parted lips and, as if hypnotised into action, she moistened them nervously with her tongue.

Stefan's breath caught on a short, smothered exclamation, then his mouth descended with tormenting slowness to cover her own. She felt her body trembling with sensations that frightened her, even as they filled her with a new and unknown excitement. He put his arms around her, gathering her close to his strength. Her trembling stopped, to be replaced by an agonising sweetness. The sure, firm touch of his mouth was inciting her to an intense longing she could neither understand nor control. Without knowing why she did it, she arched her body against his, feeling her breasts tauten as they moved against the folds of his shirt.

Suddenly he pushed her away. There was anger, mingled with passion, in his gaze. 'All right, you witch, you have won,' he said, and there was no longer any trace of kindness in his voice. 'You are a temptation too great for a saint to withstand and, God knows, I lay no claim to sainthood.'

Anna watched with inexplicable fascination as he began to strip off his clothes, tossing his shirt and belt on top of the saddlebags, and sitting down on the bed to pull off his riding-boots. 'I admit I want you,' he said. 'Are those the words you have been waiting to hear me say? You have been driving me insane with your subtle lures for the last two days.' He turned savagely and thrust her back against the prickly straw mattress. 'Tonight you can claim your victory. You have succeeded in making me forget we are enemies. But I warn you, I shall remember again tomorrow.'

Anna twisted her head, struggling to escape from his kiss. She knew that if she allowed him to capture her lips a second time, all hope of resistance would be lost. For a while, her body urged her to forget about tomorrow. He is your husband, her traitorous body whispered. Why should you not surrender to the pleasures of the moment?

With a desperate struggle she wrenched herself away from his drugging embrace and stood at the side of the bed, panting. 'And to whom are you making love, my lord Prince?' She spat out the question. 'What have you decided? Am I a madwoman? An Austrian spy? A discarded plaything of your brother, Franz?'

'At the moment, I neither know nor care. You shall be whatever you wish to be. When you are in my arms, I forget about politics, and liberty and princely betrayals. I can remember only that you are a passionate and very desirable woman, who also happens to be my wife.'

She forced herself to remain unmoved by the seductive tones of his voice. 'Your wife!' she hissed. 'An unknown female thrust upon you by Franz Johann. A woman whose name you do not even acknowledge.'

Stefan's eyes narrowed. 'You have always told me your name is Anna.' His shoulders lifted in a delicate shrug. 'If it pleases you, your name tonight shall be Anna. Come back to bed, Anna my lovely wife, and do not deny us the pleasure that waits.'

She turned her back on him, so that her eyes would not betray her. 'I am a Princess of the Carthian Royal House,' she said coldly. 'I do not bed bastard princelings, even if fate happens to thrust them upon me.'

She felt his immediate and ice-cold withdrawal without needing to turn around. She heard the quick movements with which he pulled on his discarded clothing, then heard him pick up the empty food-tray.

'The Royal Bed awaits you,' he said and his voice was filled with harsh mockery. 'Enjoy your solitary royal splendour, Princess. Believe me, I shall not trouble you again.'

Anna did not turn around until the door had slammed shut behind him. It was morning before he returned to their room.

CHAPTER
TEN

THEY left at sunrise, making their preparations for departure in virtual silence. Stefan brought her bread and hot chocolate for breakfast, but he left the room while she was eating. He returned with a pair of heavy leather shoes.

'I think these will fit,' he said.

Anna tried them on, relieved she would not have to face another day's riding without proper footwear. 'Thank you,' she said. 'They fit perfectly.'

He responded with nothing more than a brief inclination of his head. 'They were necessary. We will leave at once if you are ready.'

She sighed, not quite sure what she was regretting. 'I am ready.'

Their journey was uneventful. Even the crossing of the Brenner Pass through the mountains presented no particular problems. The early spring thaw was well past so there was no danger of flash floods, and all traces of winter snow and ice had long since vanished.

Stefan spoke scarcely at all. He offered Anna fermented apple juice at lunch-time, accompanied by some dried fruit. She noticed that he ate nothing and ventured to ask him why.

He paused for a moment before replying. 'I am not hungry.'

'We could share the dried fruit.' Anna indicated the somewhat meagre selection of shrivelled apples and raisins that composed her lunchtime meal.

'I've told you that I'm not hungry,' he snapped. She flushed and retreated into silence, and he added more gently. 'It's important you should maintain your strength. We have already spent a gruelling amount of time in the saddle.'

She guessed that he was not eating in order that she could have more food. She suspected he might be short of money and too proud to confess it. An illegitimate prince might well be hard up, she thought. She touched the pearls still clasped around her throat. 'We could sell my necklace,' she suggested. 'It would provide us with funds for several days.'

He looked at her with a strange expression then turned aside to adjust the stirrup of his mount. 'There is no need to offer me your jewels,' he said. 'The countryside is bare of food after so many months of civil war. It is not that I am without money, it is simply that the peasants are without food.'

'I see.' She hesitated, eating some raisins before she said anything more. She cleared her throat. 'I had no idea conditions in the countryside were so bad. I'm sure my fa . . . That is to say, I'm sure the old Grand Duke had no idea either. He relied too much, I believe, on Franz Johann's information.'

'You are probably right.' Stefan did not pursue the subject. 'Time to ride on, madam. Do you wish me to help you mount?'

It was late afternoon when Stefan called the final halt.

'We are here,' he said abruptly. 'We've made good time.'

Anna looked around her. The sun-baked landscape seemed deserted save for a large and imposing Italian villa, set behind a high, pink plaster wall. She searched the horizon for an inn, or a farmer's cottage, but she could see nothing. Her heart sank as Stefan directed her towards an alley alongside the villa. She was tired, but not quite tired enough to welcome the prospect of sleeping in a stable, and the alley clearly led to some sort of mews. She wondered if the owner of the Villa knew he was about to harbour the leader of the Carthian revolutionaries.

Stefan rapped sharply on an iron door set into the pink wall, and the heavy gate swung open. The elderly, white-haired gatekeeper stared at them in amazement before breaking into a delighted smile. He bowed deeply to Stefan, speaking rapidly in an Italian dialect Anna could not understand. He finished his speech by seizing Stefan's hand and kissing it.

Stefan smiled as he disengaged his hand. He gestured in Anna's direction, speaking the same dialect as the old man. To Anna's surprise, the servant immediately knelt down in the dusty courtyard and waited with his head bowed.

'What is it?' Anna asked. 'What does he want?'

'He is one of my mother's old servants,' Stefan replied. 'She gave me this estate. Gianni is welcoming you because I have just told him you are my wife.'

'Oh.' Years of training automatically took over. Anna extended her left hand towards the servant with a natural grace that ignored the state of her clothes and the dirt streaked across her face.

'Please rise,' she said in classical Italian. 'It is a pleasure to have arrived at my husband's home.'

The man got up from the floor, smiling happily as he dusted off his brown velveteen trousers. He bowed once more to Anna, seemingly not at all put out by her boyish clothes and dishevelled appearance. He stuck his fingers in his mouth and produced a startling whistle. Half a dozen grubby little boys immediately appeared, popping out from behind every pillar in the courtyard. With a great deal of enthusiastic bowing and smiling, they helped Anna dismount.

Her legs were so tired that they might not have supported her, but Stefan was already waiting and his arm was there, unobtrusive but steady as a rock, to give her the extra strength she needed.

'I will take you inside the villa,' he said. 'The housekeeper will show you to your rooms and serve you dinner in privacy. You are quite safe here. Nobody from Carthia will be able to find you.'

'Thank you.' She was too weary to question anything that he said, accepting his escort into the cool marble interior of the villa, and registering the presence of a housekeeper and several female servants through a mist of fatigue. When she saw the spacious comfort of the rooms provided for her, she had to repress the urge to fall on to the bed and sleep immediately. It seemed such a very long time since she had last been in a place of safety.

It was the sight of the bath that tempted her away from the bed. The maids conducted her into a dressing-room and pointed to the deep, china tub already filled with scented and steaming water. She was suddenly repelled by the filth of her clothes and the stench of horses which seemed to have been under her nose for longer than she could remember. With a sigh of pleasure, she submitted to the skilful assistance of the servants, emerging after some two hours with shining, clean hair, a scrubbed body and a blissful sense of relaxation. Even her legs had ceased to feel like a conglomeration of tortured muscles and now merely ached in a vague, generalised sort of way.

The housekeeper returned bearing armfuls of clean underclothing and a selection of simple, pretty nightgowns and peignoirs. Anna eyed the clothes with pleasure, although she did wonder why the villa was so well-stocked with female clothing. She decided suddenly that she was no longer tired and, ignoring the housekeeper's none-too-subtle suggestions that she should get into bed, she requested an evening dress. 'I shall dine with my husband,' she announced to the startled servant.

The housekeeper, who seemed to be the only one of the maids able to speak standard Italian, gestured agitatedly towards the bed.

'The Prince has said you are to rest, Excellency. He has told us what an arduous journey you have endured.'

Anna smiled sweetly, but there was no mistaking the determination in her voice. 'Please tell the Prince that I am very much refreshed and that I am looking forward to spending the evening in his company.'

The housekeeper appeared more agitated than ever. 'I have no dress for Your Excellency to wear.'

Anna smiled. 'Then find one,' she said and smiled again.

She was not quite sure why she did not want to go

quietly to bed. Although her body was in need of the respite only sleep could bring, her mind was restless, and her nerves tingled with a disconcerting excitement. She allowed the maids to assist her into the clean underclothes, and she slipped her arms into the prettiest of the peignoirs. When she heard Stefan's quick, angry strides in the room behind her, she knew why she had not been prepared to retire tamely to bed.

'What's this nonsensical story I hear from the housekeeper?' he asked curtly.

'I have no idea which nonsensical story you mean,' she said. Her voice was soft and demure, although her heart was racing as she turned to look at him. He, too, had taken the time to bathe and change and he was once again the magnificent stranger who had waited for her at the end of the cathedral aisle. But now, although she was even more aware of his strength, she felt no fear.

'You need sleep,' Stefan said. 'I have arranged for the servants to bring you dinner in your room.'

'I would prefer to eat with you.' She looked at him provocatively, through half-closed lashes. 'It will be our first chance to spend some time together just . . . talking. Don't you think we should get to know one another? After all, we are married.'

He drew in his breath on a quick, sharp sigh. 'I know you only too well already, madam. I repeat, you need rest and I would prefer you to go early to bed. I do not want to have your ill-health upon my conscience.' Almost against his will, he allowed his eyes to pause briefly on her face. 'I will call upon you tomorrow morning,' he said.

She pretended to acquiesce, since she saw that she would not be able to move him. 'Very well. But could I have just one or two dresses brought to me, Stefan? It is . . . humiliating . . . to have nothing to wear.'

He hesitated only for a moment. 'I am sure the servants will be able to find you something, although it will not be very fashionable.' He spoke rapidly to the housekeeper, and she nodded vigorously several times.

'Goodnight, madam.' With two quick strides he was in front of her, turning her face up for inspection, his hand placed firmly beneath her chin. 'Your face has burned in the sun,' he said at last. Again, he turned aside to issue brief instructions to the servants. His eyes rested tantalisingly upon her mouth, and she felt her lips quiver in anticipation. She did not care that the room was full of watching servants.

Abruptly, his hand fell to his side and he turned rapidly on his heel. 'Goodnight, madam,' he said again. 'Sleep well.' The door closed softly behind him and he was gone.

Anna allowed herself to be tucked into bed. She lay back against the pillows, forcing herself to ignore their welcoming softness. She smiled prettily when two of the little serving-girls brought her a tray of appetising food. They hovered attentively by her side as they indicated particular delicacies and poured out glasses of sweet red wine. She yawned, elegantly but repeatedly, between mouthfuls of food. The unsuspecting serving-girls removed her tray with polite smiles, a voluble stream of incomprehensible dialogue and a succession of bobbing curtsys. She was alone at last.

Anna waited until the sound of their giggles faded into silence before pushing back the covers and leaving the bed. She selected the simplest of the dresses the housekeeper had provided for her. Its skirts were nowhere near as full as current fashion demanded, but the pale blonde silk was flattering to her chestnut curls and, best of all, it fastened with rows of tiny buttons all down the front of the bodice. Without the help of a maid, any other style would have been impossible to put on.

She was perfectly satisfied with her appearance once she had donned the dress. Two days of boy's clothing had altered her perspective on what constituted formal evening wear. She supposed that by her former standards she looked something of a gypsy, since her skin was no longer fashionably pale but was flushed by exposure to the sun and wind. Her hair tumbled around her shoulders because nobody had thought to provide her with hairpins, but at least the riotous chestnut curls were clean. She cast a final glance in the narrow mirror and decided with relief that she did not look in the least like a boy. For some reason, she was anxious for Stefan to see that she was a woman. Fortunately for her own peace of mind, she was far too innocent to understand exactly how much she looked like a woman and how little she looked like a boy.

She descended the marble staircase. The main hallway was full of liveried servants who glanced at her curiously, but did not speak. She held her head high and walked along the corridor as if she knew exactly where she was going. Most of the doors were open, revealing empty rooms. When she came to one that was half-closed and heard the sound of low voices, she did not hesitate but flung it open and walked boldly into the room.

Professor Muller bit off a small cry of surprise.

He jumped to his feet and executed a neat bow. 'Excellency . . .' he said in a polite voice.

Stefan's chair crashed to the floor as he sprang to his feet. 'Anna!' he exclaimed. 'What are you doing here?'

She forgot her surprise at seeing the Professor and turned wonderingly towards Stefan. 'You called me Anna,' she said.

He bent down and picked up the chair. 'I asked you what you are doing here,' he said ignoring her words. 'You are supposed to be resting.'

'I am your wife, Stefan,' she said huskily. 'We have endured . . . a great deal . . . together these past few days. May I not share in your plans for the future?'

'I am a bastard princeling, madam. Of what interest could my plans be to you?'

She flushed at his evocation of the harsh words she had spoken the previous night. He could not guess how much it had cost her to insult him in such a way. 'I want to help you,' she said at last. 'There are many things in Carthia that need to be changed.'

The Professor spoke before Stefan could reply. 'Come and sit down, Princess. You must be tired, for my friend Stefan has been telling me something of your magnificent courage over the past few days.'

She was grateful to the Professor for his kindness. She knew Stefan could not really have been praising her, but she appreciated the courtesy of Professor Muller's encouraging lie. She smiled a little shakily and slipped into the chair next to the Professor. 'I want to help,' she repeated, amazed at her own determination. 'I don't think Franz Johann should be allowed to govern the people of Carthia by the force of his army alone.'

'What are you suggesting?' Stefan asked sarcastically. 'Are you about to proclaim your belief in parliamentary democracy? Or do you merely wish to substitute a dictator more to the Austrian taste than Franz Johann?'

'I think Carthia should have a parliament. I think my fath . . .' She saw his lowered brows and corrected herself hastily. 'I believe Carthia needs a parliament and a constitutional monarchy.'

'Let us stop this charade now,' Stefan muttered between clenched teeth. 'Don't attempt to divert us any more with your false protestations. Stay, if you will, for unlike Franz Johann I have no stomach for locking people in their rooms. God knows, there is little damage you can do to our cause from here.' He turned back impatiently to the Professor. 'Finish telling me about the ambush at Georg's farm. How many of you escaped?'

'All, save Georg.'

Stefan's face twisted with pain. 'So many men have sacrificed their lives and for *nothing*! We must make arrangements to take care of his wife and daughters. Not that any pension from me can ever replace such a devoted husband and father.'

'His wife will be grateful to you, nevertheless.'

'You know better than to mention my name in the matter. You also know that the money comes from my mother's estate and can only be used for charitable purposes. I am not even being generous to Frau Georg with my own funds.'

Professor Muller rested a hand on Stefan's arm. 'Do not berate yourself so, my friend. You were not responsible for Georg's death. No. If there is any blame to be apportioned, it should be placed at my door. I recognised Hans's hatred of the aristocracy and I failed to take adequate precautions. Of course, it was Hans who betrayed us by summoning the soldiers. I should have guessed weeks ago what he was planning to do and I should not have allowed him to take part in the rescue of you and your bride. I included him because he was such an excellent rider and knew the local terrain so well.'

'What do you mean, rescue?' Anna asked.

The Professor smiled tolerantly, patting her hand. 'You surely do not still believe that we abducted you, my dear? Stefan smuggled letters out of Franz Johann's prison, and told us that whenever his carriage was seen leaving Innesbad it was to be stopped. He knew his brother's word could never be trusted, you see. So naturally we made arrangements to stop Stefan's carriage. We knew all his servants—every last one of them—had been murdered and replaced with the lackeys of Franz Johann's choosing. We had to rescue you both, therefore, while the odds of success were still in our favour.'

Stefan interrupted before Anna could ask any more questions. 'What has been done about Hans?'

'He was taken to Genoa and put on a boat leaving for the United States of America. He can do us no harm across the Atlantic and, perhaps, in a country without nobility, he will rid himself of his hatred sufficiently to use the brilliant intellect God gave him.'

'So what are we to do now?' Stefan paced the room restlessly. 'I feel so frustrated, thwarted at every turn! I dare not make any move that will precipitate a violent reaction by my brother. Heaven knows, the people of Carthia could not survive another two years such as they have just endured. We are at peace and must strive to remain so. Our plans must not involve the peasants, Professor. We must contrive to force Franz Johann to abdicate.'

The Professor smiled wryly. 'Then I shall pray even more fervently that God is on our side, for I confess that there is no plan which springs into my mind which will achieve our goals.'

'Franz Johann will never abdicate,' Anna said. 'He will cling to his throne even if it brings the whole of Carthia down about his ears.'

The Professor spoke quietly. 'You seem remarkably sure of your judgment, Princess.'

'I know Franz Johann,' she replied. 'And Stefan must also know in his heart that what I say is true. The Grand Duke will never voluntarily give up the power he has schemed and murdered to achieve.'

'And yet you fell in with his plans for you with scarcely a whisper of protest,' Stefan said harshly.

Anna looked at him, her eyes clear and steady. 'I was beside myself with grief that night. I scarcely knew what was being said. And anyway, what would you have preferred me to do? Should I have defied him and condemned us both to a needless death?'

'My friends, this is no time to be arguing over the rights and wrongs of the past. The future presses all too closely upon us. Franz Johann has announced that he must put aside his personal grief and marry, so that the Duchy may have an heir. Soon we shall not only be struggling against Franz Johann, but a son trained in his image.'

'Surely even my brother would hesitate to bring an Austrian into the country just at this moment,' Stefan remarked. 'And there is no noble family in Carthia which would permit their daughter to marry such a notorious pervert, even if the marriage would make the girl Grand Duchess.'

'It is never wise to under-estimate Franz Johann. He has already found a Carthian bride. He is to wed the Princess Luisa, younger sister to Anna Teresa, his murdered fiancée.'

'No!' Anna heard the scream of protest rip from her throat, but she couldn't control it. 'Oh, poor little Luisa, what are they making you do?' She pushed her chair back, turning to seize the Professor's hands as if she could force him to retract his story. Her breath came out of her lungs in great heaving gasps and she knew her face must be deathly pale. 'Tell me you have invented this tale,' she pleaded. 'It is just a rumour, is it not? The Dowager Grand Duchess would never agree to such a match while she and Luisa are still in deep mourning!'

'Princess, you must calm yourself,' said the Professor. Gently, he pressed Anna back into the chair. 'I fear the story is true. The official announcement was made to the Council of Ministers two days ago and copies of the proclamation were circulated to the mayors of every town. The wedding will take place in less than two months, and it is easy to understand why. You can see how advantageous such a match is for him. Luisa has inherited all her parents' unentailed wealth and all her sister's dowry. Moreover, although the old Grand Duke was not a clever man, he was basically well-meaning. There is a residue of respect for him and for his family among the peasants. Franz Johann needs an alliance with that family, and Luisa is the only daughter left.'

'He shall not marry her!' Anna was beside herself with panic. She scarcely knew what she feared most. It was intolerable to think that her sister might be forced to live as the wife of the man who had murdered her parents. It was almost worse to wonder if Franz Johann was preparing to eliminate yet another member of her family.

'I must go!' she exclaimed wildly. 'I must leave. I must warn Luisa!' She was beyond rational thought and she clutched at Stefan's arm, forgetting he was her enemy and remembering only how swiftly he had dealt with the problems of the past few days. 'You must take me back to Carthia,' she said. 'Why didn't I think of it before? I must ride back to Carlsberg and see my grandmother. The Dowager Grand Duchess will know what to do.'

'Stop it!' Stefan commanded, his voice low and clipped with the effort of control. She could feel the rigid muscles of his arm beneath her fingers before he pulled his arm roughly away. 'Why have you returned to that foolish masquerade? What is all this pretended panic because Franz Johann announces his plans to marry?' His eyes narrowed and he looked at her with sudden suspicion. 'Is it possible that this distress is real? Don't tell me that you love that perverted monster! Have you no idea how he treats those few women who are unlucky enough to be brought into his bedroom?' Stefan's face paled until it was as white as her own. 'If you were one of his women, surely to God you did not *enjoy* the experience?'

Anna felt sick. 'It's you who are mad! You and

your crazy revolutionary friends.' The tears she had struggled to contain overflowed on to her cheeks, but she was too desperate to wipe them away. 'I'm leaving here whether or not you will take me. I shall seek out the Dowager Grand Duchess and put an end to this charade. I should have done it before!'

Without stopping to say another word, she turned and ran out of the room, rushing along the high-ceilinged marble corridors and up the stairs to her room. Her eyes were blinded by tears and she ignored the calls she heard coming from the Professor.

She hunted for her discarded riding-breeches, ripping the dress off her shoulders as she searched. She heard the door bang open and Stefan stormed into the room. He was alone. He slammed the door shut and strode over to her. She stared at him mutinously and he shook her fiercely. 'What do you think you're doing, you crazy child? You don't have the sense of a two-year-old! You can't ride out, alone, at this hour of the night. Don't you realise you are irrational from lack of rest?'

The urgency which filled her drove all caution out of her mind. 'Luisa is my *sister*,' she said savagely. 'Do you expect me to rest while she is handed over to a monster? Have you forgotten that Franz Johann is the man who murdered my parents and forced me into marriage with you?'

Stefan's face was white to the lips. His eyes were filled with violent anger and another emotion Anna could not interpret. 'I will stop that delectable mouth of yours from uttering these preposterous lies!' he breathed. 'If I cannot achieve your submission in one way, I shall achieve it in another.' He forced her head round, holding it tightly so that she could not move and his mouth descended to cover her lips in a burning, passionate kiss. At first, she was too surprised to struggle and gradually, as his lips continued to caress her, all desire to escape him left. She forgot why she ought to defy him as her body melted into the crushing strength of his embrace.

Stefan lifted his mouth for a second and looked at her, a strange glitter masking the deeper emotion in his gaze. 'Witch!' he muttered softly as he kissed the nape of her neck. 'Enchantress . . .' he murmured against her lips.

She made some incoherent reply, parting her lips as she pressed herself against him. He gave a sound, something between a groan and a curse, then lifted her into his arms and carried her across to the bed. For a moment she was filled with fear and she glanced up at him, panic darkening her eyes.

'Do not look at me so,' he whispered. 'Anna, you have won the battle. I am insane with the desire to feel your body submitting to mine. Enjoy your triumph while it lasts, because tomorrow I shall force myself to remember that I am a revolutionary and that you are an enemy of my people.'

She did not understand anything that he said, but she no longer cared. How could he talk of victories and enemies when his mouth was turning her body to fire in his arms?

'I love you, Stefan,' she whispered and, as she surrendered herself to the power of his passion, she wept because she knew her words were true.

CHAPTER
ELEVEN

WHEN she awoke the next morning, she was alone in the great bed. She searched for Stefan but there was no sign of him in any of the rooms of her suite. All trace of his presence seemed to have been removed, so that the events of the previous night might have been nothing more than a wild, sweet dream.

But she knew Stefan's love-making had been all too real. Her body quivered with a new awareness of passion. She suspected that if Stefan walked into the room, her heart would leap with excitement at the prospect of welcoming him back into her arms. She told herself that she could not—would not— love the man who had led the fight against her father, but her emotions betrayed her reason. She was hopelessly, irretrievably, in love.

She asked the servants where Stefan might be found but they could not understand her questions. When, in desperation, she mentioned the Professor's name, a young servant-girl led her to Professor Muller's room.

He greeted Anna with his habitual courtesy. 'Come in, my dear Princess. How may I be of service to you this morning?'

'Where's Stefan?' she asked. Her emotions were so badly jangled that she found it difficult to imitate the Professor's good manners.

He gestured to a chair and saw that she was comfortably seated before replying. 'I haven't seen Stefan this morning, my dear. He did not return to our meeting last night.' He noticed Anna's heightened colour and said gently, 'Was there some special reason why you wish to see him so urgently?'

'No . . . Yes.' Anna drew in a deep breath and summoning all her courage looked drectly into the Professor's eyes. 'Professor, answer me honestly, if you please. Do I appear mad to you?'

'No.' His response was swift and unequivocal.

'Your life has depended many times, it must have done, on your assessment of people's characters. You must have learned to judge when people are speaking honestly. Will you listen to me, Professor, and forget everything Stefan has told you about me? Will you judge me as though we were meeting for the first time, and your life depended upon your decision?'

Professor Muller was silent for a while. When he spoke, he looked at Anna with a small, wry, smile. 'I will offer you the courtesy of replying honestly, my dear. It is not easy for any man, even one as old and withered as myself, to listen to you and judge you objectively. Your appearance, Princess, does not make it easy for men to retain a cool head and a clear sense of judgment in your presence. My friend Stefan has, I know, driven himself to the limits of his endurance in forcing himself to remain immune to the . . . attractions . . . of your person.'

'My family never used to say I was particularly beautiful,' Anna said unhappily. 'And it is unfair that just because you and Stefan think I am pretty that you should doubt everything I say.'

The Professor laughed ruefully. 'I don't think

pretty is quite the word Stefan would use to describe you, my dear. But what you say is true to a certain extent. It is unreasonable of us menfolk to listen attentively to my daughter merely because she is plain, and to ignore your words simply because you are beautiful.'

'Is your daughter very upset at losing Stefan?' Anna asked. 'Truly, Professor, Stefan and I had no choice. Our marriage was thrust upon us as a life-and-death matter.'

'I am sure it was,' the Professor said. 'And Maria is certainly not suffering from a broken heart—any more than Stefan is. Maria admires the Prince because she shares his political views. She would have been proud to become his wife and help in his task of bringing justice to the Carthian people. Now she has decided to go to England next month, where I have no doubt she will soon forget him. She did not love Stefan as you do.'

'Is it so very obvious that I love him?'

'To me it is, although perhaps not to Stefan. We can sometimes be particularly blind to the things that are most important to us.'

Anna drew in another deep breath. 'Well, if you can see that I love Stefan, perhaps you will be able to see that I would have no reason to lie to him about my identity.'

'What are you trying to say, my dear?'

'Professor Muller, I am the Princess Anna Teresa. I was in the carriage when my parents were assassinated and, partly because of the prompt actions of my father and partly because of sheer luck, I survived the assassination attempt. I am not mad when I say this. I am not trying to deceive you with some subtle plot. If you will persuade Stefan to take me back to my family's castle in Carlsberg, the Dowager Grand Duchess and my sister Luisa will undoubtedly recognise me. If you know any intimate details concerning my family that might not be public knowledge, test me. I swear to you, that I am the Princess Anna Teresa.'

The silence in the room stretched out unbearably.

'If you are indeed the Princess Anna Teresa, how did you come to be held captive in Franz Johann's castle?' the Professor finally asked. 'And why on earth would he have buried a false Anna Teresa when he had the real one under his nose? Why didn't he kill you when he arrived at the scene of the massacre?'

'I escaped from my parents' carriage and ran away into the woods,' she said quickly. 'My cousin must have been furious when he discovered I was gone, so he buried my lady-in-waiting, claiming that she was the Princess Anna Teresa. Perhaps he hoped I would never turn up again. Perhaps he planned all along to deny me if I ever reappeared in Carthia, I don't know.'

'But you have not answered me completely. Why, having escaped Franz Johann's clutches, did you run straight back into his power? Why, in God's name, did you run to Innesbad Castle of all places?'

Anna laughed bitterly. 'I was a naïve young girl three weeks ago, Professor. Franz Johann was my cousin and my promised husband. I did not like him, but I did not believe him capable of such gross treachery as the murder of my parents. I ran to him because I thought he was my refuge.'

'Why would Franz Johann murder your parents?

After all, everybody knew that the old Grand Duke was no more than a puppet dancing to Franz Johann's tune. Franz Johann was the legal heir, and he was about to marry the eldest daughter of the reigning Grand Duke. His position was unassailable. He had little to gain and, potentially, much to lose in murdering his relatives.'

'His position was not as unassailable as you think, Professor. My mother was expecting the birth of a child in October. Franz faced the birth of a son who would be the new direct heir. For this threat to his prospects, he was prepared to wipe out my whole family and twenty or thirty court servants.'

'So that was the reason for the attack!' the Professor exclaimed. 'We had all wondered.'

'You believe me? You believe I am telling the truth?'

'It is . . . difficult . . . for me to change my mind so suddenly. But what you say has the ring of truth to it. Forgive me, my dear, but I *must* ask you some more questions. It seems inconceivable to me that Franz Johann should have made the massive blunder of marrying the real Princess Anna Teresa to Prince Stefan.'

'Why do you call it a blunder?'

'Anna Teresa is heir to all her parents' personal estates. She is the eldest direct descendant of a line that has ruled Carthia for four hundred years. True, she is a woman and Carthia will not accept a woman as reigning Grand Duchess in her own right, but it is dangerous for Franz Johann to have such a centre of power outside his control. Stefan, for his part, is the leader of a powerful opposition party. Can you not see what a potentially explosive situation Franz Johann has created? Why should he allow two such grave potential threats to marry?'

Anna's brow wrinkled in concentration. 'I have thought about my cousin's motives. He knew very well that I was Anna Teresa, so his decision wasn't taken in ignorance of the true facts. I think he felt we were less threatening tied to each other than we were separately. He introduced me to Stefan in such a way that Stefan inevitably assumed that every word I uttered was a lie. Franz hinted repeatedly that I was mad, or if not mad then at least corrupt. Stefan certainly believed him. Then my cousin spread the rumour that I was an Austrian and that rumour severely lessened Stefan's popularity with the Carthian people. Perhaps Franz Johann hoped Stefan would be cast aside as leader of the revolutionaries. Perhaps he even hoped the rebels would murder us both, thus saving him the dangerous task of planning another assassination of two popular people.'

'It is possible, I suppose. It is certainly possible . . . And that is why you were so distressed at the news of Princess Luisa's betrothal?'

'She is my sister, Professor, and not yet sixteen. I can't let her marry Franz Johann, knowing as I do that he murdered our parents. My grandmother thinks of marriage simply as a political weapon and she may have advised Luisa to accept the match. As for Luisa herself . . . Well, she is young. Marriage is still a game to her, and she would like to be Grand Duchess of Carthia. She enjoys dressing up and would think only of jewels and new ballgowns and parties. She is too young to see that Franz Johann is a monster in human disguise.' Anna smiled bitterly. 'Three weeks ago, I was also too young.'

Professor Muller stood up and bowed deeply. 'You have endured a great deal over the past week, Your Highness. I trust you will accept my apologies for any pain or discomfort I may unwittingly have caused. I also ask you to accept the heartfelt sympathies of a loyal Carthian subject on the death of your parents.'

Anna's eyes filled with tears. 'Thank you, Professor, for your trust in me.' Her breath caught on a sob, quickly smothered and changed into a rather wavering laugh. 'You had better sit down. It seems somewhat absurd to stand upon rules of etiquette. It also says a great deal for my experiences over the past few days that I believe you when you claim to be a loyal subject of Carthia.'

The Professor gestured earnestly as he sat down. 'Princess, the world is changing around us with lightning speed. Railways are starting to criss-cross Europe; men are leaving the countryside to work in factories. Half the citizens of Carthia can now read and write. The people are informed concerning the march of world events and they deserve a voice in the decisions taken by the Carthian government. Stefan did not seek to overthrow your father's rule. He merely wished to make the Grand Duke answerable to a freely-elected parliament of Carthian citizens. He did not precipitate a revolution, Your Highness. He did everything in his power to control the peasants and to make them understand that they would be the losers if they resorted to violence. He begged the Grand Duke to make concessions before it was too late, but his pleas were in vain. Franz Johann had already poisoned your father's mind.'

'My father was a good man at heart, I believe,

but he was not . . . very clever. Franz Johann, on the other hand, possesses a brilliant mind and he manipulated my father to the detriment of the Carthian people. I have been taught to accept every detail of the hereditary principle of government and the absolute authority of the monarch. It isn't easy for me to cast aside nineteen years of training, but I don't believe, any longer, that Franz Johann should be allowed to reign as Grand Duke even though he is the legal heir. He is a murderer, and he should be treated as we treat any other murderer. He must be tried and punished for his crime.'

The Professor was once again silent for such a long time that Anna wondered if he had begun to doubt her story. His voice was clear, but very low when once he did speak again.

'What do you think will happen to the Carthian government if we succeed in exposing Franz Johann as the assassin he is?'

'Why . . . well . . . I had not thought so far. The next in line will inherit.' Her brow creased in worry and surprise. 'It is extraordinary, but I have no idea who is the heir after Franz Johann. It is very strange that the subject should never have been discussed. Miss Frobisher, my governess, was so particular in informing me of the constitution and history of Carthia.'

'Stefan is the next heir,' the Professor said.

'Stefan! But he is a bast . . . That is to say, surely he is not eligible to inherit?'

The Professor did not answer her question. 'I think I may know where to find Stefan,' he said with a sudden air of decisiveness. 'It is very hot outside, Your Highness, and the carriages in this part of the world are usually open. May I suggest that we send a maid to find you a hat with a veil to protect you from the road dust, and also a parasol to protect you from the sun?'

'Let us by all means,' Anna said with a slight smile. 'I must learn to think like a lady again, and strive to forget that I have spent the past few days tearing over Central Europe on horse-back, sleeping in rebel hideouts and smugglers' dens.'

'Your Highness is, if I may say so, a very remark-able young woman. And my friend Stefan is a very lucky man.'

Anna blushed. 'I am not sure he appreciates his good fortune,' she said wryly.

"You read his character as badly as he reads yours,' said the Professor with a smile. 'Come. It is time we started to sort out this tangle.' He pulled sharply on the bellpull. 'For the first time in months, I am hopeful for the destiny of Carthia,' he said. 'I think, Your Highness, that you will find the visit we are about to make of great interest.'

The Professor was silent during their short drive, unwilling to talk and apparently lost in some com-plex train of thought. Anna was quite glad of the silence since it gave her time to compose mentally what she would say when they encountered Stefan. How, she thought, did one approach an indifferent husband when you had discovered you were madly in love with him?

'I think Prince Stefan will be at the Convent of Santa Maria di Vittoria,' said the Professor break-ing his long silence as they approached a building almost hidden behind its high, encircling wall. A nun guarded the gates of the convent. She did not speak or even smile at them as they drove up, but she seemed to recognise both the carriage and the servants' livery. She asked the coachmen no questions, but simply waved them all inside the tiny mud-paved courtyard.

The interior of the convent was white-washed, bare of ornamentation and silent. There was no sign of a school or a hospital, so it seemed likely the nuns were members of one of the contemplative orders dedicated to unceasing prayer. Anna felt oppressed by the utter quiet as the Professor ushered her into a small antechamber.

'Wait for me here,' he instructed her.

'Do you know this convent well?' Anna asked, although it was evident that the Professor had visited the convent before.

'Yes. I have known it for several years. Please wait, Your Highness. I shall send Stefan to you.' He disappeared behind an iron-grilled doorway and Anna was left alone in the empty room with nothing to do save stare out of single barred window on to the blank wall of a whitewashed outbuilding.

Stefan appeared suddenly in the main doorway. The Professor was not with him. Instead, he was accompanied by an elderly, white-garbed nun, whose face was obscured by a wide starched wimple. Anna scarcely gave the nun a second glance, for her attention was riveted upon her husband.

'G-good-morning,' she said, all the clever conversational gambits she had prepared flying right out of her mind.

'Good-morning.' She could sense Stefan's tension, although she could not guess at its cause.

'Why have you followed me here? What do you want?' he asked.

'Professor Muller brought me. Hasn't he explained why we came?'

'He tells me you have something important to say to me. He has urged me to listen with an open mind.'

'I hoped the Professor would come back . . . It would be easier to explain if he were here . . .'

'He seems to think we would deal better alone,' Stefan responded curtly. Almost to himself, he added, 'God knows, I attempted to persuade him otherwise.'

Hesitantly, Anna glanced towards the silent nun. 'But we are not alone. Does the holy sister speak our language?'

Stefan laughed without any sign of genuine mirth. 'Are you learning discretion at last, my dear wife? It has come a little late, I fear. But you need not worry about . . . the holy sister, as you call her. You may say whatever you wish in front of the nuns of this convent. They are vowed to silence and have dispensations to speak only in very special circumstances. You run no risk that your confidences will become public knowledge. Besides, there are reasons why I wish this particular nun to remain with us. What do you need to tell me so urgently?'

Ann twisted the stem of her parasol somewhat helplessly between her fingers. 'It was the Professor who seemed to think it was essential to come,' she said. She wished Stefan would not scowl at her with a fierceness that made her knees shake, even though her body still ached with the memory of the passion they had shared such a few short hours ago. She felt her face flame with the warmth of remembered desire, and she spoke quickly, before her expression could betray any more of her secret emotions.

'This morning . . . you weren't there . . . That is to say, when I couldn't find you, I sought out the Professor.' She drew a deep, steadying, breath and forced herself to look straight into Stefan's accusing grey eyes. 'I thought it was time . . . I thought events were getting out of hand. I wanted to tell him who I am. I told the Professor I really am the Princess Anna Teresa and I explained to him exactly how I escaped death at Franz Johann's hands. The Professor believed me, that's why he brought me here.' She dropped her gaze hastily, so that she could protect herself from the blaze of anger which leapt into Stefan's eyes. 'He thought you should know right away,' she said defiantly. 'He thinks Franz Johann has committed a blunder in allowing us to marry. Perhaps the blunder can be turned to your advantage, although I admit I don't exactly see how.'

The nun suddenly ceased her silent contemplation of the floor. 'You did not tell me your bride was so beautiful,' she said in perfect, classical Italian. A note of amusement crept into her musical voice. 'The strange gaps in your recent conversation with me now become comprehensible.'

Anna was shocked to hear the nun speak, and Stefan seemed equally surprised. The nun walked towards Anna with noiseless steps. When they were very close, she lifted her head so that the wimple no longer concealed her features, and Anna was able to see what a handsome woman the nun must once have been. The fine bone structure remained unimpaired, enhanced rather than obscured by the stark severity of her habit. Her deep grey eyes examined every detail of Anna's face and, after a long scrutiny, she gave a small, sweet smile.

'Anna Teresa, dear child,' she said, speaking in the high German of the Carthian court. 'You are very like your mother, although you are more beautiful than she ever was . . .'

'You recognise me!' Anna's breath came out in a long sigh. 'Oh, thank God! Somebody knows me at last!'

'Your mother and I grew up together. As I said, you are very like her.' For a moment the nun's eyes were lit by a teasing, silent laughter that turned the serenity of her face into the image of the vivacious, passionate woman she must once have been. 'However,' she said, 'Your hair comes straight from Eugenie, your French grandmother. I suspect you have her temperament to match the fire of your hair. Am I correct?'

'My governess often complained of it, Sister.' Anna's smile was rueful. 'But my life over the past few weeks has been too chaotic to allow me time to indulge in temper tantrums.'

Stefan was staring at Anna as if he had been turned into a block of stone by the nun's words. 'Oh my God!' he muttered. 'What have I done?'

'Nothing very terrible, I imagine,' said the nun. 'I am so glad, Anna Teresa, that the Professor brought you here.'

'It is wonderful to meet with someone who knew my parents well, Sister. And yet I do not know who you are.'

'I would like you to introduce me to your wife, Stefan.'

He came forward stiffly, as if only by holding his body rigid could he keep a check on the emotions seething within him. 'This is my mother,' he said and the words fell like chips of ice into the pool of silence. 'She is also the Dowager Countess of Styria and Innesbad, and the Dowager Baroness of Bruchwald.'

'It is true I am your mother,' the nun intervened gently, 'But I no longer use those other titles. I am simply a member of the Order of Santa Maria di Vittoria. Anna Teresa, it is my pleasure to welcome you as a daughter in my family.'

'But I thought you were dead!' Astonishment drove all the normal courtesies out of Anna's head.

Stefan's mother smiled. 'I might say the same about you, my dear. But here we both are, very much alive.'

'Why did my parents never encourage us to meet?' Anna asked. 'Why have I always thought you were dead? Franz Johann always spoke as though his mother had been dead for years.'

Stefan made an involuntary movement, and colour suffused Anna's cheeks. In the stress of meeting Stefan's mother, she had forgotten that this nun must be the same notorious woman who had, according to Franz Johann, taken numerous lovers and eventually given birth to Stefan, an illegitimate child. 'I'm sorry,' she stuttered. 'I did not mean to pry into matters that are no concern of mine.'

The nun's face showed no trace of anger. 'I would like to tell you a little about my husband, who was a good man and deserved a better wife than I.'

Stefan interrupted. 'There is no need to distress

yourself with these old tales, Mother.'

The nun corrected him gently. 'Anna Teresa is your wife,' she said. 'Don't you think she is entitled to hear the truth?'

'I explained to you how we came to be married. I don't see any need for you to speak of matters you would prefer to forget.'

The nun—how difficult it was to remember that she was mother to both Stefan and Franz Johann, Anna thought—inclined her head in a brief acknowledgement of her son's concern, but she looked at Anna when she began to speak.

'My husband, the Count of Innesbad, was a kind-hearted man, many years older than I. Our marriage was arranged when I was seventeen and I had every intention of being a dutiful, loving wife. In fact, I was looking forward to becoming a countess. A year after Franz Johann was born, my husband was sent as a military envoy to the Austrian court and he was ordered to leave me behind.

'Two weeks after the Count left for Vienna, a new British Ambassador arrived to take up residence at the Carthian court. He was everything my husband was not: young, handsome, witty and charming. By the time of our second meeting, we were deeply in love.' For the first time, the nun's face showed signs of stress. 'Even now, after all these years, it isn't easy to call my feelings for Richard sinful. What we felt for each other seemed to transcend the normal moral laws and we became lovers within days of our first meeting.'

'Mother, I can explain all this to Anna later— another day. Please don't torment yourself in this way.'

The nun smiled sadly. 'It is not a torment for me to remember Richard. On the contrary.'

'I would like to hear what your mother has to say, Stefan.'

'It is probably your right,' he said harshly. 'I suppose that as a Princess of the Carthian Royal House you are entitled to explore the pedigree of the dubious princeling to whom you find yourself tied. Irrevocably, after last night.' He saw the nun's face turn white and he cursed softly beneath his breath. 'I'm sorry, Mother. I did not intend to hurt you.'

The nun looked at Anna and she could see the plea for understanding that lurked beneath the nun's outward serenity.

'Tell me about Stefan's birth,' she said softly. 'Please, Sister.'

'Stefan was born almost eleven months after my husband left for Vienna. Even if Richard and I had wanted to lie, deception would have been impossible. From the hour of his birth, Stefan's appearance stamped him as Richard's son. I was banished from Carthia and Richard was recalled to London in darkest disgrace. King William IV was not the stern moralist that Queen Victoria is proving to be, but even he could not quite stomach his ambassador conducting a notorious love affair with the wife of the Carthian heir apparent. It says much for the Count of Innesbad's generous nature that he took no steps to punish either Richard or me.'

Stefan placed his arm around his mother's stiffly-held shoulders. 'I beg you not to distress yourself further,' he murmured.

The nun's grey eyes, so like her son's Anna realised, darkened with a hint of rueful humour.

'Confession is good for the soul, is it not? I want your wife to understand the situation, Stefan. The future of Carthia is at stake.' She turned back to face Anna. 'Richard and I lived together in England for twenty years. When Richard died ten years ago, I knew my own life was virtually ended. Stefan inherited all his father's estates in England, so his future was financially secure. I arranged to enter this convent.' For a moment, the wry, sophisticated humour flashed again in the nun's eyes. 'When we cannot repent in the privacy of our souls, we sometimes feel the need to make extravagant gestures of public repentance.'

Anna spoke hesitantly. 'I daresay, Sister, that God has forgiven many worse sinners than you.'

'Oh I expect God has forgiven me for my adultery long ago. It is my intolerable pride which will keep me racked in Purgatory. However impressed the world may be by my hair shirts and simple cotton gowns, God is not deceived.'

'You don't have to explain anything more to me, Sister,' Anna said. 'I do understand . . .' She thought to herself that she understood only too well how love could overcome years of training and discipline.

The nun smiled gratefully. 'I still have to warn you about Franz Johann, for he is the true burden of guilt I have to carry. When he was a baby, I neglected him in order to spend time with Richard and then, when he was old enough to miss me but too young to understand anything of his parents' troubles, I went to England. Franz Johann never received the love he should have done, and his life has been built upon hate and bitterness. I neglected him, and produced a monster. Stefan tries to shield me from the truth, but it's amazing how much one can hear in an out-of-the-way convent in a forgotten corner of Italy. I know that Franz Johann is a cruel man, and a murderer who is unfit to rule Carthia. And his crimes can be laid at my door.'

'In the end, we are all responsible for our own actions,' Anna said quietly, aware that Stefan's gaze was fixed on her.

His mother looked from one of them to the other, her eyes resting briefly on Stefan's rigidly compressed mouth and Anna's flushed cheeks. 'Do you have any questions, Anna Teresa?'

'Professor Muller told me Stefan was heir to the Grand Dukedom of Carthia after Franz Johann. Forgive me, Sister, but I don't understand how that can be. You said yourself that Stefan's father was an Englishman.'

'The law, my dear, does not always recognise biological reality. When a woman is married, her children are presumed to be her husband's offspring unless the husband formally denies parentage. My husband, the Count, had no desire to increase the scandal surrounding my banishment from Innesbad and he never legally denied Stefan's legitimacy. My husband was a kind man and a shrewd judge of character. He saw the failings in Franz Johann as clearly as anybody else. When I entered this convent, the Count summoned Stefan to Carthia. It didn't take my husband long to decide that Stefan was a more promising heir to the Duchy than Franz Johann. He made Stefan into his chief advisor, confirmed him in the rank of Prince and on his death bed officially proclaimed that Stefan was his son. My husband hoped that Franz Johann would turn to his half-brother for advice, and that

Stefan would moderate Franz's wilder flights of autocracy. I'm afraid, however, that Franz has merely allowed his original resentment of Stefan's popularity to grow into an obsessive hatred.' Abruptly, the nun stopped speaking.

'I have said enough. You have the documents you came to find, Stefan. Make what use of them you will.'

'Come back to Carthia with us,' Stefan said. 'It is your home.'

She cut him off with a sharp gesture. 'My place is here in this convent. I am vowed to obedience, Stefan. That vow, at least, I can keep.' She returned her hands to her sleeves, concealing her long, aristocratic fingers in the folds of rough white cotton. 'Goodbye, my dears. I shall pray for the success of your efforts in Carthia, and for the safety of you all, including my poor neglected Franz . . .'

'Mother . . .'

She turned and gave Stefan a final, dismissive smile. 'No, Stefan. I can do nothing further which you would consider useful to aid your cause. I can only pray, which may be the greatest help of all.' Her dark grey eyes rested for a long moment on her son's face before turning to look at Anna.

'Take care of Stefan for me,' she said. 'He is more precious to me than he ought to be, and he will assuredly take no care of himself.'

Before Anna could reply, the nun had opened the iron-grilled door and was gone.

CHAPTER
TWELVE

'It seems, madam, that I have an almost infinite number of reasons to apologise to you,' Stefan said with extreme formality. 'It is too much to hope that you will be able to forget my . . . ungentleman-like . . . behaviour. I can only ask you to accept that too many months in Franz Johann's dungeons clouded my judgment more than I knew.'

'What are you talking about?' Anna asked quietly.

'The fact that you are the Princess Anna Teresa of Carthia,' he said curtly. 'Above all, the fact that I did not even try to listen when you told me who you were. Last night . . .'

'What about last night?' Anna kept her gaze averted. Her heart was pounding and she guessed her feelings must be clearly written on her face. She didn't want Stefan to pretend to love her. It was certainly not his pity that she wanted.

'I bitterly regret the events of last night, madam,' Stefan replied. 'God knows, I should have been capable of resisting temptation.' His face was white when he spoke again. 'If you wish to apply for an annulment of the marriage, I will swear that last night's consummation was forced upon you.'

'Last night you called me Anna,' she said irrelevantly.

There was a long pause. She could hear the

cicadas squeaking outside the narrow window. Stefan's gaze seemed fixed upon a speck of dust on his polished boots. 'Last night we both said many things that I am sure you would prefer to forget this morning.' He looked at her at last, and she stood perfectly still while he subjected her features to close scrutiny. 'My mother was right, of course,' he said. 'You are the image of the former Grand Duchess, although your colouring is different. I must have been wilfully blind not to see the similarities.'

'It is easy not to see those things which contradict our preconceived notions. I should know, because I have spent the best part of nineteen years ignoring the evidence of my eyes.'

'What does that mean?'

'It means that I wish to help you in your plans for Carthia,' Anna said. She wished he would not hide behind his façade of determined formality. It was hard to believe this cool, remote man was the same person who had made love to her with such passion the previous night. Even if he did not love her, surely he must at least like her. Or did words murmured in passion have no validity in the harsh light of day?

'I think it would be unwise for you to seek an annulment of our marriage,' she said.

'Why?'

'You are the legal heir after Franz Johann,' she said quickly. 'If he is found guilty of the murder of my parents—as he must be when I give evidence—surely it would be a political advantage for you to be married to me? After all, I am the daughter of the previous Grand Duke of Carthia.'

'I have made far too much use of you already,

madam. I married you in order to save my life and I don't intend to hold you to this mockery of a marriage simply because it would prove politically useful to me and my revolutionary friends. I still retain . . . some shreds . . . of honour.'

'I wish you would stop calling me *Madam* in that ridiculous way. My name is Anna as I have been telling you for some days now. I wish you could bring yourself to use it,' she said.

'Your Highness is too generous. It is better if we both forget the false intimacies Franz Johann forced upon us. You are too innocent to know what you are sacrificing.'

'You are a fool, Stefan, and I don't intend to ruin my life because of your misplaced chivalry. What do you suppose I shall do with my life if this marriage of ours is annulled? Who shall I marry now? How shall I explain that it is no virgin bride who comes to him, but a woman who has been shown how to make love?' She saw how troubled Stefan looked, and she pressed her advantage. 'Franz Johann compelled us to marry, it is true, but is that not all the more reason to turn our marriage into a weapon that can defeat him?'

'Perhaps so.' Stefan hesitated visibly. 'If you would care to remain here in this convent until conditions in Carthia are more settled, I should be happy to return eventually and claim you as my wife.'

'You mean, if you are successful in your claim to govern Carthia, I may share in your triumph. But if Franz Johann wins, I can stay here and fade into gentle obscurity? Is that how you intend to treat your wife, Stefan? As a helpless doll, to be displayed when some state occasion requires the feminine touch? Have you forgotten that I am the woman who has vowed to support you through every difficulty? I am your *wife*.'

'Damn it, that does not mean you are required to lay your life on Franz Johann's chopping-block for a second time in the space of two weeks! Anna, I beg you . . . That is to say, I do not see that any useful purpose can be achieved by your return to Carthia at this point.'

'Then I hope Professor Muller can persuade you to see otherwise, because I fully intend to return. I want to see my grandmother and my sister Luisa. It's past time they learned that I am not dead.'

'I will not escort you into danger.' Almost to himself he murmured. 'Not again. I have done that too often these past few days.'

She felt herself come alive at this evidence of his concern for her. Was it possible that what she had to fight against was not Stefan's indifference, but his exaggerated sense of honour? 'Which would you prefer?' she asked slowly, almost afraid to put her new ideas to the test. 'Do you want a fight to the death with Franz Johann that might cause all of Carthia to plunge into civil war? Or do you prefer a simple, personal confrontation which will show him that by surrendering the dukedom, he can save his life?'

Stefan's expression was entirely unreadable until a reluctant smile appeared at the corners of his mouth. 'Do you always get your own way, Anna?'

Her heart turned over when she saw his smile. 'Not always,' she said.

'But you knew I could not resist your offer when you expressed it in such terms. What is your plan?'

She sighed with relief that her point was virtually

won. 'I'll tell you when we are in the carriage. I shall faint from weariness if I have to stand up in this empty room much longer.'

'I don't believe you. After observing you over the past few days, I am convinced you have more strength of will than most men twice your size.' Nevertheless, Stefan held out his arm to support her and Anna rested her hand against the strength of his forearm. Her slight shiver of physical awareness as soon as they touched was already familiar to her, as if she had known it all her life, just as was the answering tension of Stefan's muscles.

He looked down at her, and she could have sworn there was a reluctant tenderness in the depth of his eyes. 'The Professor will be waiting for us,' he said.

'Then let's hurry,' she replied and walked quickly out of the silent convent into the warm sunshine.

It was dawn the next day when their carriage rattled into the outer courtyard of the Grand Duke's castle in Carlsberg. Once through the mountain pass, Stefan had harnessed four hired horses to the shafts, changing teams every five or six hours so that their travelling time had been reduced to a bare minimum. He drove the team of horses with only one servant from his Italian estate to share the long hours at the reins. Anna and the Professor remained inside the coach.

On this occasion, despite the risks involved, they were forced to travel along the main highways, since the coach could not have traversed the rough paths Stefan and Anna had followed on their outward journey. Although they encountered several small troops of Carthian soldiers, nobody stopped the gilded Italian coach with its ecclesiastical crest painted on the door panels. In fact, they accomplished the journey with such ease that Anna felt a superstitious fear as they halted at the massive gateway of her previous home. She shrank back into a shadowy corner of the carriage when Stefan, dressed in the robes of an Italian priest, leaned down from the driver's seat and shouted out to the guard on duty at the gate.

'I have documents concerning Princess Luisa's marriage to deliver to the Dowager Grand Duchess of Carthia. We have come directly from His Holiness in Rome.' He spoke in a German tainted with the lilting vowel sounds of Central Italy and the guard inspected their carriage without suspicion and with barely a flicker of interest.

The great iron gates were swung open on the guard's command. Two of the soldiers even managed a half-hearted salute as the carriage rolled quickly across the cobbled forecourt and into the inner courtyard. Grooms ran out to assist in the stabling of the horses. Anna, in the black habit of a Benedictine nun, stood silently beside the Professor while Stefan repeated their story to the officer of the watch. If the duty officer felt any curiosity as to why a heavily-veiled nun was part of an ecclesiastical messenger party, his curiosity was insufficient to make him question the evidence of several papal seals prominently displayed on Stefan's documents. As they were escorted into one of the castle antechambers, Anna reflected that for a royal castle in a country recovering from a violent revolution, security left a great deal to be desired.

Once they were inside, their progress into the

presence of the Dowager Grand Duchess was unbearably slow, although no more difficult to achieve than their original admittance. Despite the elaborate screening process, none of the self-important castle clerks ever really doubted that the two priests and the silent nun were exactly what they seemed. The interminable delays were merely a ritual the officials performed so that each could make an entry into his ledger and proclaim, with a flourish, that his duty had been performed. Anna began to wonder why she and her family had not been murdered in their beds at the beginning of the revolution.

At last they were in the presence of the personal secretary to the Dowager Grand Duchess. He was polite, but bored.

'I will hand your papers immediately to Her Highness, the Grand Duchess. Perhaps, Father, you and your . . . er . . . travelling companions . . . would care to step into my private sitting-room and I will see that you are provided with refreshments. I assume you will be spending the night in the home of the bishop . . . the archbishop . . . ?' He allowed his voice to tail off into a question.

'We wish to speak personally with Her Highness, the Dowager Grand Duchess.' Stefan allowed his gaze to roam over the motionless lackeys stationed at various points in the room. He lowered his voice to a murmur. 'The documents, sir, are a mere pretext. We have a special message to deliver to the Grand Duchess. Please warn her to be prepared for a great shock.'

His words were carefully chosen, thrashed out in discussion with Anna and the Professor. Her grandmother was a strong woman, but Anna did not want her to arrive expecting to grant a routine audience to a papal courier, only to find herself confronting a granddaughter she had believed to be dead. The shock might well have disastrous consequences.

The secretary looked flustered. He was not accustomed to coping with deviations from the established routine. 'Father, I cannot permit you to disturb the Dowager Grand Duchess unless I know the precise nature of your business.'

Anna stepped out of the shadows, tugging at her veils as she did so. Her hair fell out around her shoulders in a rippling cascade of chestnut. There was an audible gasp from the footmen and the secretary turned first white, then green.

'Good morning, Herr Block,' Anna said calmly. 'I am sorry we had to deceive you. As you can imagine, it was impossible for us to gain admittance any other way.'

The secretary's mouth hung open. He snapped it shut.

'You are dead,' he managed to say at last.

'No,' Anna replied with a small smile. 'I'm very much alive. Will you fetch my grandmother? We will explain everything to her. And Herr Block, please warn her of what she can expect to see when she comes into this room.'

The secretary, still decidedly green about the gills, backed out of the room bowing deeply. Stefan spoke to her abruptly. 'Are you all right?' he asked.

'Yes.' She drew a deep breath. 'It's good to be home. I feel as though I have been away for a hundred years.'

Stefan flinched, but she did not have time to wonder why her words had provoked such a strong reaction. Her grandmother whirled into the room, her skirts rustling with the force of her anger.

'Where is the impostor?' she said fiercely. 'I shall have her in prison before the day is over! How *dare* she!'

Anna dipped into a curtsy before reaching up to kiss the Dowager's cheek. 'It is I, Anna Teresa, Grandmother.' She would not admit, even to herself, how her mouth had become dry with fright and how her knees trembled. What if her grandmother was like Franz Johann and either could not or would not recognise her? 'Please say that you are glad to see me,' she said.

'Anna Teresa,' the Dowager whispered. '*Oh, Anna! Ma chérie, c'est vraiment toi. Tu n'es pas morte . . .*' She swayed, and Stefan held out his arms to stop her falling. Gently, he led her to a chair and helped her to sit down. Anna quickly crossed the room and knelt by her side.

'Grandmother, have I frightened you? You only speak French when you are very happy or very angry. I hope this time you are very happy.'

A faint trace of colour returned to the Dowager's cheeks. 'Anna,' she said softly and allowed her hands to trace the outline of her granddaughter's face. 'I am very happy,' she said as two tears rolled down her cheeks. 'Very, very happy,' she repeated.

Anna nestled her cheek in her grandmother's hand and gave a small sigh of contentment. 'Grandmother, there is so much to tell you, so much to explain, and we have driven all night to get here. May I . . . may we talk to you alone?'

The Dowager began to recover something of her normal poise. 'I was forgetting the priests who were good enough to bring you to me,' she said. She stood up and extended her hand graciously towards the Professor.

'I am very much in your debt, Father, and yours too, Father.' She smiled at Stefan. 'I know you will understand why I feel the need to be alone with my granddaughter. But I shall hope to see you later this evening at dinner, and express to you my profound gratitude for your deeds. I shall send a messenger to the bishop, asking him to join us.'

Anna spoke uncomfortably. 'Grandmother, you don't understand. These men . . . They are not priests . . . I . . . we . . . have something to say to you. Could I not talk to you alone?' she finished desperately.

'But we are alone,' said the Dowager, mystified. 'Except for Herr Block.' The Dowager gestured elegantly to her secretary. 'My dear sir, you will forgive us, I know. Perhaps you could seek out the Princess Luisa and inform her of the good news we have to give her? She could join us in an hour, perhaps?'

Herr Block once again bowed himself out of the room and the Dowager settled herself more comfortably in the chair. 'Now,' she said. 'We are quite alone. What have you to tell me, little one? Oh! I still can't believe the happiness of having you with me! To think you escaped those wicked revolutionaries! Outwitted them, I have no doubt. And your cousin Franz Johann! How thrilled he will be to discover you are alive! He has spoken to me so many times of his grief at your death.' A sudden frown flickered across the Dowager's smoothly-painted brow. 'Hmm . . . there is the question of Luisa's betrothal. We shall have to decide what to do.'

'The footmen,' Anna interrupted. 'Grandmother, there are still five footmen in the room.'

The Dowager looked up with some astonishment, as if just recognising that the five pillars of red and gold velvet were human beings and not pieces of furniture. With the air of one humouring an invalid, she shrugged delicately.

'You are dismissed,' she said to the footmen.

Anna sensed the disappointment of all five servants as they filed out of the room. They had been hoping to stay and hear her story, she realised. How was it impossible that for nineteen years she had lived surrounded by servants without being aware of their feelings? With a faint pang of regret, she knew that she had changed irreversibly during her days with Stefan. Much as she loved her grandmother, their old relationship could never quite be restored.

'Grandmother,' she said when the door closed behind the last of the footmen. 'Grandmother, I have already told you these men are not priests.' She swallowed hard. 'I would like to introduce my rescuers to you. They have saved my life and I know you will be as grateful to them as I am. This is Herr Doktor Muller, Professor of Philosophy at the University of Carthia. And this is Prince Stefan of Innesbad.' She paused uncertainly. 'He is . . . He is my husband.'

'*Prince* Stefan! Your *husband*! *Oh, mon Dieu!* But do not worry, my dear child, it shall be annulled.' She looked more closely at the Professor as he raised himself from a deep bow and her face flushed darkly with anger. 'Professor Muller! Anna, how could you bring that scoundrel, that lying revolutionary, into my presence? Oh, my little one, what have they done to you! How have they forced you into these despicable acts?'

Anna turned pale with the force of her grandmother's anger, which was every bit as fierce as she had expected. She was grateful to feel the support of Stefan's arm around her waist. The firm pressure of his fingers against her side warmed her, although the rest of her body felt icy-cold. Stefan spoke calmly to the Dowager, his face once again covered with the mask of impassivity that he had worn when Anna first met him. It was his protection, she realised with a sudden flash of insight. It was his defence against a sensitivity that made him far too vulnerable.

'Your Highness need not fear that the Princess Anna Teresa is being held to our marriage against her will,' he said. 'She has decided for the sake of our country to honour the vows she made to me last week. I beg Your Highness to listen to what your granddaughter has to say. If you cannot trust me, I hope you will have sufficient confidence in Anna Teresa to know that she could not lie.'

'Very prettily spoken, *Prince* Stefan,' the Dowager sneered. 'Is that how you persuaded so many fools at the Innesbad court to forget that you are a bastard?'

Stefan turned white, but he did not attempt to defend himself and Anna turned passionately upon her grandmother. 'Stefan is a true prince of Innesbad. The Count, Franz Johann's father, declared his legitimacy before he died. Stefan has the papers to support his claim and, in law, he is the heir to the Dukedom after Franz Johann.'

The Dowager was silent for a long time. 'Well, at least he has brought you back to me. We shall see about these other matters. But later on . . .'

'Grandmother, you can't ignore Stefan's claim to the Dukedom. Nor can we pretend our marriage never took place.'

'*Mon Dieu!* Now I recall!' the Dowager interrupted. 'Stefan was married to an Austrian noblewoman only a week or so ago. How could I have forgotten? Poor little Anna! He has managed to deceive you with some false wedding ceremony.' The Dowager scrutinised first Stefan and then her granddaughter with piercing shrewdness. 'And it is too late for an annulment, is it not? He has tricked you into consummating this false marriage?'

'I have already promised Anna Teresa . . .' Stefan began stiffly.

Anna interrupted him. 'Yes,' she said ruthlessly. 'It is too late for an annulment and I do not wish for one anyway. But you have not understood, Grandmother. Stefan did not marry an unknown Austrian noblewoman. He married me. I was the girl in the cathedral last week. Franz Johann forced us to agree to marry, or he threatened to kill us both.'

'Franz Johann?' The Dowager sank deeper into her chair. Her body, normally so upright, seemed to wither visibly. 'I do not understand,' she said. 'You talk nonsense and bring revolutionaries into my presence. I no longer understand anything.'

'Your Highness,' Stefan said quietly, 'I beg you to listen to us carefully. For the sake of Carthia's future, you must understand. It was when Anna Teresa heard of her sister's engagement to Franz Johann that she insisted upon returning here right away.' His voice dropped a little as he continued. 'God knows, I have no wish to bring her back into such danger. If I had followed my selfish inclinations, I would have carried her a thousand miles away from Carthia and all its troubles. I have estates in England. There is no need for her to subject herself to this danger.'

'You must not worry about your sister's betrothal,' the Dowager said, replying only to the first part of Stefan's remarks. 'We did not know you were alive, Anna Teresa, and so her marriage seemed a political necessity.'

'I'm not offended because Franz Johann wanted to marry Luisa,' Anna replied impatiently. 'I am simply terrified for my sister's safety. You must accept the fact that Franz Johann knows I'm alive. You can't possibly pretend that he married me to Stefan in the cathedral while ignorant of my identity. I know Franz Johann is your grandson, but I can't keep silent about what he has done. It was he who ordered the assassination of my mother and father. The murderers were Franz Johann's hirelings, not revolutionary fanatics. I survived the assassination attempt so I have first-hand evidence of his treachery. I saw it all.'

The Dowager held up her hand. 'Do not speak so,' she said hoarsely. 'Marriage has unhinged your reason. Do not continue to tell me these crazy lies.'

Anna looked at her grandmother and pity softened her mouth into tenderness. She saw the network of lines that wrinkled the Dowager's face, deepened over the past few weeks so that no paint could now disguise their presence. She also saw how the Dowager's hands trembled until she clasped them tightly together in her lap.

'Too many people recently have tried to pretend that I'm mad,' Anna said. 'Why should I lie? Why should marriage to Stefan unhinge my mind? Am I so fragile? You know very well that Franz Johann had a motive for the crime. He was afraid that my mother would give birth to a baby boy and then Franz Johann would no longer have been heir to the dukedom. If you did not fear his reaction, why did you and my father insist upon announcing my betrothal before you told him my mother was going to have a baby?'

'It was because of the presence of the Austrian troops,' the Dowager said hurriedly. 'We wanted them to report to the Austrian Emperor that everything was under control in Carthia again. We wanted them to know the future of the royal house was secure.'

'Was that the real reason?' Anna asked. 'I believe that both you and my father feared Franz Johann's reaction to the news of my mother's pregnancy. I believe you used me and my betrothal as a bribe to pacify him, to prevent him causing trouble if the baby happened to be a boy. He is your grandson, Grandmother, and my father's nephew, but deep inside your hearts you both knew that he was an ambitious and scheming man who would stop at nothing to obtain absolute power in Carthia.'

There was a long silence in the room. 'What are you going to do?' the Dowager asked at last, her voice scarcely more than a thread of sound. 'Franz Johann is the rightful Duke of Carthia and I will not lend my support to any usurpation of his rightful authority.'

'The right of hereditary succession does not give a man the right to murder and lie his way to the throne,' Stefan said quietly. 'I ask you to remember, Your Highness, that Franz Johann killed your son, your daughter-in-law and your unborn grandchild so that he could call himself Grand Duke of Carthia. Are you sure you can't help us to force his abdication?'

'There is no other immediate male heir,' the Dowager objected. 'Carthia would be plunged into chaos if Franz Johann abdicated.'

'That is only because there have been so many questions about my legitimacy,' Stefan said quietly. 'Your Highness, I agree with you that I have no hereditary right to the Grand Dukedom of Carthia. My true father was an Englishman, therefore I am not the biological son of the former Count of Innesbad, although he was kind enough to honour me on his deathbed with the legal protection of his parenthood. But Anna Teresa has four hundred years of Carthian royal blood in her veins. By a chain of almost unbelievable circumstances, fate has decreed that we should find ourselves married. I have the legal documents to prove my claims as heir to the Dukedom. Anna Teresa has the biological right to be Grand Duchess. Do you not think that, for the good of Carthia, you could support our claim? Our country can't survive many more years of rule by Franz Johann. He is a man guided only by hatred and an insane lust for personal power.'

The Dowager looked at Stefan intently. 'Fine words, sir, but I know all about your rabble-rousing past. What of your revolutionary friends? Where do they fit into this rosy picture of Carthia's future?'

'Unless this country is given a parliament, I guarantee that within a generation it will have devoured itself in civil war. I intend to appoint Professor Muller Prime Minister of our first parliament,' Stefan said defiantly. His face relaxed into a faint shadow of a smile. 'There is nothing like incorporating a rebel into the governmental process if you wish to temper his revolutionary ardour.'

With something of her old vigour, the Dowager stood up and gestured imperiously towards the silent Professor. 'So it comes to this! You are expecting me to deny my grandson his rightful place at the head of the Carthian government so that a bastard prince and a bourgeois revolutionary may take his place?'

The Professor spoke for the first time. 'You are a great patriot, Your Highness, and a very clever woman. Therefore, that is precisely what we are expecting you to do.'

CHAPTER
THIRTEEN

PRINCE Franz Johann of Innesbad, Grand Duke of Carthia, was in a foul mood. Three hundred hand-picked soldiers had been scouring the countryside for traces of Stefan and Anna Teresa. So far they had encountered nothing save a multitude of sullen peasants. Anna and Stefan had apparently vanished into thin air.

He crumpled the latest report into a ball and tossed it aside angrily. He was honest enough to curse himself for his earlier misjudgment. He should have executed the pair of them while he had them under his roof and to hell with the consequences in the country. He could always have pretended Stefan was shot while trying to escape.

Beneath his anger, Franz Johann was aware of a nagging fear that was all the more unpleasant for being less than completely rational. What, after all, could Stefan and Anna Teresa actually do to him? They could never get into Innesbad castle, Colonel von Drucker would see to that.

His plans had seemed so perfect. By forcing Stefan into marriage he cut off a dangerous alliance with Professor Muller and discredited Stefan in front of his supporters. As far as Anna Teresa was concerned, there had been an element of sadistic personal pleasure in ordering the marriage. Anna had never respected him as she should, and it was exquisitely pleasurable to imagine her condemned as a ranting madwoman when she tried to claim her true identity. Of course, it was doubtful if her sanity would hold up under the weight of so many unaccustomed burdens and then he would have the satisfaction of knowing that his half-brother was married to a lunatic.

On a more practical level, Franz Johann had filled Stefan's estate with carefully trained spies and surrounded it with soldiers. A week ago he had been confidently looking forward to hearing that Stefan had been recaptured and the documents found. Those damned documents that proclaimed the unwelcome fact of his brother's legal rights and—even more damaging—explained just why the old Count of Innesbad did not think Franz Johann was fit to rule in Carthia.

A week ago, he had expected to hear at any minute that Stefan and Anna Teresa had been 'accidentally' killed following capture. He had arranged any number of alternative accidents for the tiresome couple. He had not expected Stefan to make contact with his former revolutionary friends but, just to be on the safe side, he had ordered the student, Hans, to organise an ambush. That ambush had somehow been badly bungled and Hans had disappeared. Franz Johann did not even know if Stefan had ever been at the farm.

The spies disguised as servants on Stefan's estate had been supplied with three different varieties of quick-acting poison, but poison was of no use if Stefan and Anna Teresa weren't there to consume it. The soldiers had been ordered to shoot if Stefan were seen anywhere near his estate. So far, he hadn't been within twenty miles of its boundaries.

So all Franz Johann's careful plans had come to naught. He had gambled on retrieving those cursed papers his fool of a father had signed, and he had lost. Not only the papers, but Stefan and Anna Teresa as well. The tiny fear began to grow again. What if Stefan ever found out that his wife was truly a Princess of the Carthian Royal House? What if Anna Teresa managed to make contact with some of her family before she was driven mad? Franz Johann broke out in a cold sweat of fear. He had forgotten to increase the guards on Carlsberg Castle. Franz Johann pushed the fear away. No woman could possibly survive the wrenching shocks Anna Teresa had endured. On her wedding-day, he had seen that she hovered on the very edge of collapse, clinging to her sanity with a faint but stubborn obstinacy . . . Nevertheless, he would increase the guard on the castle at Carlsberg as of tonight. No point in risking her gaining access to that tiresome old Dowager. Not that anybody on the run—not even Stefan—would ever risk escorting a woman he scarcely knew right into the enemy stronghold.

It was impossible, of course, that Anna Teresa would survive the rigours of a full week spent on the run. And Stefan, in any case, would not listen to her stories or pay much attention to her pleas. If only he could feel sure Stefan would abandon her . . . kill her if the going became too rough. But Stefan was such a sentimental fool . . . Always determined to protect people who were weaker than himself . . . Never realising that in this world it's only the cruel and the strong who survive. All in all, Franz Johann decided, it had been a very bad mistake to marry Anna to Stefan. They were a potentially dangerous combination.

'What is it?' Franz Johann scowled ferociously at the guard who appeared at the entrance to his room.

'An urgent message from the Dowager Grand Duchess of Carthia, Your Highness.'

Franz Johann took the letter, his anger fading slightly. At least his betrothal to Luisa remained a bright spot in the surrounding gloom. She was a silly girl, not as pretty as her sister, but that did not trouble Franz Johann. He was not very interested in women, beautiful or otherwise, and it was pleasant to spend time with Princess Luisa. She so obviously considered him a genius. He slit open the heavily crested letter. The Dowager was nothing like her remaining granddaughter. She was a tough old bird if ever there was one. And in many ways Anna Teresa took after her grandmother. They shared more than just the colour of their hair.

Franz Johann read the letter, his lips relaxing into a smile. For whatever reason, the Old Lady was clearly anxious to get this betrothal firmly tied up. She was asking for a full meeting of the Carthian Council, together with the presence of the Archbishop, so that the betrothal arrangements could be concluded and an early date for the wedding agreed upon. Franz Johann thought of the first instalment of Princess Luisa's dowry and smiled. He rang the little golden bell at the side of his desk. The Grand Duchess would be arriving in Innesbad late the next morning. He glanced up as his secretary came into the room. 'Send messages to all the Councillors of State,' he said. 'There will be a meeting in the Grand Council Chamber of the castle at three o'clock tomorrow afternoon. Summon the Archbishop as well. We shall be completing the arrangements for my marriage to the Princess Luisa.'

'Yes, Your Highness.'

Franz Johann watched the slim retreating back of his secretary. He was a new recruit and a good-looking man. His golden hair looked soft and . . . Franz Johann dragged his mind back to the Grand Duchess's letter. He'd marry Luisa at the end of next week and then he could say to hell with Stefan and that damned aggravating Anna Teresa. He'd make sure Luisa produced a child nine months after they were married and if it wasn't a boy . . . well, he knew how to take care of that problem. There were plenty of lusty male babies born every day in Innesbad.

Franz Johann rang for some wine. The footman was relieved to see that for the first time in several days his master was smiling.

The Council Chamber was full when the Grand Duke Franz Johann entered it precisely at three. He had heard that the young Queen Victoria had pronounced punctuality to be the courtesy of kings, and he now prided himself on his punctuality. He bowed perfunctorily to the Archbishop of Carthia and nodded even more cursorily to the remainder of the councillors.

'My lords,' he said. 'The Dowager Grand Duchess of Carthia and Her Highness, the Princess Luisa of Carthia will be here shortly. I received word that they arrived in the castle over an hour ago. As my messengers informed you yesterday, the Dowager Grand Duchess has requested this meeting to ask for your co-operation in making plans for my immediate marriage to the Princess Luisa.' He kept his eyes carefully lowered and managed to infuse a certain huskiness into his voice. 'Whatever my personal feelings, the security of Carthia has to be my first consideration. We have decided that an early marriage is necessary for the stability of my country.'

He sensed the murmur of approval that came from the right-hand side of the long table. The older, more conservative councillors always sat together and they were willing to offer him whatever support he required provided that he could keep order in the restless countryside. The younger councillors, some of them educated in England or France, were always less easy to win over. He risked a quick, upward glance and saw the Archbishop staring at him with a cynical wisdom that belied the other-worldly dignity of his cardinal's robes. He and the old Dowager were a shrewd pair whom it would be wiser not to under-estimate. The Archbishop, damn him, was not beholden to the Grand Duke of Carthia for his power and he had come close to siding openly with Stefan and the rebellious peasantry during the revolution. The days when kings and rulers could count on the unquestioning support of the Church were unfortunately over. Franz Johann allowed his mind to wander into a pleasant daydream about the appointment he would recommend to the Vatican when the Archbishop finally died. He felt the Archbishop's eyes resting on him with hidden amusement, and he had the sudden, acutely uncomfortable feeling that the Archbishop had read his mind. He was inordinately relieved when the herald announced the arrival of the Dowager, the Princess Luisa and the party of attendants.

The Dowager stood in the doorway while the councillors rose to their feet and bowed deeply. Princess Luisa, as was proper, remained slightly behind her grandmother. They were both clothed in deep mourning, but their heads, necks and arms gleamed with diamonds. The old lady, Franz Johann thought, was putting on a marvellous show. She was attended by the usual cluster of court officials, and also by a small military guard-of-honour, which was somewhat unusual.

'Please be seated, my lord councillors.' The Dowager's voice had never lost its seductive French intonation. Franz Johann's gaze flicked cynically over the older councillors, wondering how many of them had been the Dowager's lovers. Her love affairs had been widely suspected, but discreetly conducted. Not like his mother with her single-minded obsession for the Englishman. Franz Johann snapped his thoughts to a close. He was allowing his mind to wander far too frequently these days. He supposed it came of trusting nobody and talking to nobody honestly save himself.

He smiled and walked quickly down the length of the table towards the Dowager. 'Welcome, my dear grandmother. Welcome to Your Highness.' He raised her hand and kissed it gracefully. 'Princess Luisa, it is my pleasure to welcome you on your first visit to Innesbad.'

She was too shy to meet his eyes and dropped a slight curtsy. She really was a silly little thing, he thought. 'As you requested,' he said to the Dowager, 'the Council is assembled.'

'I am pleased,' nodded the Dowager. She smiled.

'I have brought some visitors with me from Carlsberg. I think the councillors will be most interested in what they have to say.'

A premonitory chill raced along Franz Johann's spine.

'Visitors?' he queried.

'Yes,' said the Dowager. 'Somebody you have professed to love so often, I know you will be pleased to see her.' She dropped her gaze, but Franz Johann was not deceived. Before she veiled them, he saw that the Dowager's eyes were darkened by a revulsion she could scarcely conceal.

There was no longer any pretence of holding a routine meeting. The councillors were craning their necks towards the door in their eagerness to see who had accompanied the Dowager and Princess Luisa. The Archbishop moved away from his chair and quietly positioned himself closer to the Grand Duke's side.

One of the court attendants cast aside the dark cloak she had been wearing. There was a rustle of silk, the swish of heavy skirts as Anna Teresa curtsied to the Archbishop.

Franz Johann heard the gasp of mingled fear and astonishment that rose as a single sound from the assembled councillors. He tasted the vile sourness of vomit in his throat but he did not allow the sickness to overcome him. He watched Anna Teresa as she walked slowly, regally, to the head of the table.

She was dressed in the blue silk gown she had worn for their betrothal ball. Her throat was a blaze of sapphires. A tiara, more like a small crown than an ornament, nestled in the luxurious copper curls of her hair. For a long time, Franz Johann's gaze

rested on her with the hypnotised intensity of a
rabbit confronted by a stoat, then, with a
tremendous effort, he pulled his eyes away, only to
find himself confronted by the tall, black-clad
figure of Prince Stefan.

It was the personification of his worst nightmares. He clutched his throat, but no sound
emerged and Stefan looked at him pityingly. It was
the same, all-encompassing pity that invariably
reduced Franz Johann to a state of impotent fury.
He wanted Stefan to fear him, not pity him. He
found his voice at last. 'What are you doing here?'
he hissed. 'Why did you bring these traitors here?'
he said to the Dowager, struggling to bring his voice
under control. 'They are impostors! Anna Teresa is
dead. I buried her! I did!'

Without looking at her cousin, Anna Teresa
spoke to the Archbishop. Her voice was low, but so
crystal-clear that her words were audible in every
corner of the room.

'I am asking you, Monsignor, to take note of a
miracle. I am not claiming, of course, to have
returned from the dead. I am only claiming that I
survived the death by assassination that Prince
Franz Johann planned for me. My parents and the
twenty-eight members of our party were not so
fortunate.'

The Archbishop managed to make himself heard
over the immediate outcry from the councillors.
'You are making grave accusations, Your Highness. The Grand Duke has shown us convincing
proof that the attack was mounted by revolutionaries.'

'I survived the attempt because my parents protected me with their bodies,' Anna Teresa said. 'I

saw the assassins. They were not revolutionaries; they were Carthian soldiers.'

Franz Johann managed to inject a convincing sneer into his words. 'Anybody may dress as a Carthian soldier,' he said. 'Where is your evidence for these terrible accusations?' He hurried across the room and came to stand at Anna's side. 'My dear,' he said softly, 'I understand how you must have suffered these past few days wherever you have been hiding. But come, I am your cousin as well as your fiancé. May we not talk things over quietly together?'

There was a murmur of approval around the Council table. Even the younger, more radical members of the Council appeared relieved. It was one thing to oppose the Grand Duke on the grounds of his autocracy. It was another to face up to the possibility that he was a multiple murderer.

Anna Teresa still did not raise her voice. 'What do we have to talk about now, Franz, that we did not have before? You have known for days that I was still alive.'

'Of course I have not,' he blustered. 'That's a foolish statement, Anna Teresa.'

'Shall we fetch Colonel von Drucker, so that he can tell the Council what happened while he was on guard duty one night two weeks ago?'

'No!' Franz Johann smiled tightly. 'My dear, there is no point in trying to justify your delusions. You have allowed your excellent judgment to be warped by the tragedy of your parents' death. In the circumstances, I am willing to overlook your wild accusations.'

Prince Stefan spoke for the first time since entering the Council chamber. 'Perhaps, then, Franz

Johann, you would care to explain how you arranged a wedding ceremony between the Princess Anna Teresa and myself? That must have been rather difficult to do, since you did not know she was alive . . .'

The Archbishop looked up quickly. 'Are you saying you married the Princess Anna Teresa?' he asked, not disguising his incredulity. 'Prince Stefan, we both know that I myself married you to an Austrian noblewoman.'

'No, Monsignor. You married me to Anna Teresa. She was forced by my brother to use a false name but such a ceremony is still valid. You could not see my bride clearly through her lace veils, but Franz Johann knew very well who she was. He had already buried a lady-in-waiting and claimed she was Anna Teresa, so he needed to provide the true Princess with a fresh identity before he killed her. Once we were married, he banished us to my estates where, I have no doubt, he had prepared some clever scheme for killing us both. Thanks to some of my friends we were able to avoid his traps and—after a certain amount of difficulty—we have returned to tell you the story.'

Franz Johann's face was purple with fury. 'Lies, all lies!' he exclaimed. He turned towards the councillors and spread his hands wide in a gesture of appeal. 'My lords, I beg you to consider. Stefan has told you a preposterous tale! He claims that he is actually married to my cousin. Very well. We will not talk of the deception they practised when I arranged the ceremony for them. I forgive them. I do more. I wish them every happiness. This meeting, if you recall, was summoned to confirm my betrothal to the Princess Luisa. Let us go ahead and arrange that wedding, and forget about Stefan's. The future security of Carthia is at stake. The Duchy needs a direct heir. What do you think would happen in the countryside, my lords, if you attempted to depose me and proclaim another ruler? Do you remember that the next heir is a distant relative, descended from a brother of my great-grandfather. He lives in Vienna and is a leading member of the Imperial court. Do you seriously propose to install an *Austrian* as the next Grand Duke of Carthia? Do you wish to *invite* the peasants to rebel?'

'Your genealogy is at fault,' Stefan intervened quietly. 'You must know, Franz, that I am the next heir to the Dukedom. And I am a Carthian, not an Austrian, married to the elder daughter of our last Duke.'

'You are a scheming bastard.' Franz Johann scarcely managed to produce the insult through his tightly-clenched lips.

'No,' Stefan replied. 'I have the documents, witnessed by a priest and sealed by the Archbishop of Carthia, which bear my father's seal and his official, legal confirmation that I am a legitimate offspring of his marriage with our mother.'

'Damn the documents! They are forgeries! I have had all your estates surrounded ever since my father died! Not a fly could have got into any of them, so you can't have retrieved those cursed papers from there. These documents are forgeries!'

'The documents were not hidden in Carthia. My father sent them for safe-keeping to his wife.'

'She's dead!' Franz Johann yelled.

Stefan allowed himself a small, weary smile. 'You seem to have considerable difficulty in sorting the living from the dead, Franz. Our mother is very much alive. She has written to you many times over the years, but you chose to ignore her letters.'

The Archbishop came forward. 'To my certain knowledge, the former Countess of Innesbad is alive,' he said. 'I have already seen these documents, Prince Stefan, as you know. May I show them to the other members of the Council?'

'The Dowager Grand Duchess is carrying them. We felt it was safer so.'

Franz Johann knew the precise moment at which his control snapped. The Archbishop turned away to speak to the Dowager and Franz was left confronting his brother: tall, handsome, *hateful* Stefan who had stolen their mother's love and then come home to steal the affections of the old Count, who wasn't even Stefan's father. And now he had won Anna Teresa's heart! She was looking at Stefan with the same sickly revolting adoration his mother had shown to that treacherous Englishman. And he, Franz Johann, had been the man who caused them to meet and fall in love.

He felt the rage force its way up from the pit of his stomach, hardening and sharpening until it became a steel rod of fiery pain wound round his throat. The room faded to blackness. All he could see was the pale oval of Stefan's face, taunting him with its strength and self-assurance.

'I'll kill you!' he cried, although he was not sure if the words emerged over the band constricting his throat. The pistol from inside his jacket was in his hand, the silver shaft gleaming with a molten fire that matched the fire within him. He lunged towards Stefan, trying to push away the blackness.

'You are a bastard!' he croaked as he raised the gun. 'Everybody ought to love *me*.'

He heard the screams and knew they were not his own, but the darkness was all-enveloping and he did not care. He felt the bullet rip from the weapon in his hand, piercing the darkness so that for a shining moment he saw Stefan's face twisted into a mask of terror. Franz Johann smiled. Now they will all love me, he thought.

'Anna! Oh my God! Anna!' There was no mistaking the anguish in Stefan's voice and Franz Johann smiled again. The steel band was gone, his throat no longer hurt. He sat down on the floor, nursing his shiny silver pistol.

'Mama?' he said, peering intently through the darkness. There was a warm, silk-clad body on the floor and he lay down next to it.

'Mama.' He repeated the word with a contented sigh as the darkness crept up and covered him.

CHAPTER
FOURTEEN

ONE of the elderly councillors slumped forward on to the table in a faint. His head made a banging noise as it cracked against the solid mahogany of the conference table. A second councillor rocked back and forth in his seat moaning 'She's dead! Anna Teresa is dead!' When nobody attempted to deny the truth of his assertion, he proceeded to chant it with an hypnotic, repetitive rhythm. 'She's dead! Anna Teresa is dead! Oh heavens, the Princess is dead!'

Stefan knelt by the side of Anna's inert body, pressing his handkerchief in a pad against the wound. He had already ripped the shoulder seam of her dress in a single, ruthless movement and revealed the gaping slash where the bullet had passed. 'Do you have another handkerchief?' he asked the Archbishop.

'Is she badly hurt?' the Archbishop asked as he handed over a large, white silk square.

'No,' Stefan replied tersely. 'Send somebody for a doctor, will you? And for God's sake stop that lunatic from moaning!' He recalled that he was addressing a Cardinal of the Church, and apologised. 'I beg your pardon, Monsignor.'

The Archbishop had not waited to hear the apology. He had already crossed the room and stood in front of the wailing councillor. 'Ferdinand, old fellow, shut up, will you? Try not to be more of a fool than is inevitable. The Princess Anna Teresa has a slight shoulder wound.'

The councillor spoken to thus brusquely stopped his chant with amazing promptness. The Archbishop made sure that a footman had already been despatched to find the palace doctor, then he turned back to the councillor. 'I suggest that you tend to your neighbour,' he said, pointing to the inert form of the other councillor who was still slumped over the table.

The Dowager Grand Duchess had meanwhile walked the length of the room and stood stiffly at Stefan's side.

'How is she?' asked the Dowager.

'A surface wound only. The bullet grazed her shoulder.' Stefan moved Anna's body fractionally and pointed out a scar in the polished wooden floor. 'You can see where the bullet has lodged itself.'

The Dowager swayed and sat down rather heavily in a nearby chair. Princess Luisa knelt at her grand-mother's side, her face a pale shade of grey.

'I was afraid,' the Dowager said at last.

Stefan glanced up momentarily and a gleam of mutual understanding passed between the two of them. 'So was I,' he said simply.

Anna gave a groan. Her eyelids fluttered, then became still again. Stefan lifted her head so that it rested more comfortably against his supporting arm. 'Anna?' he asked softly.

There was no reply. 'Where is that fool of a doctor?' he asked of nobody in particular. 'Didn't anybody tell him this was *urgent*?' Tenderly, he brushed her hair back from her forehead. 'Anna, my dearest, please wake up,' he said softly.

Her eyelashes immediately fluttered open. 'What did you say?' she asked, her violet eyes fixed upon Stefan.

'I said, "Why the devil are you still unconscious?"'

'Oh . . .' She sighed and closed her eyes. 'I feel very weak . . .'

Before Stefan could reply, the Dowager knelt beside her granddaughter. 'Anna, my dear child, are you in great pain?'

Anna struggled to sit up. She was perfectly content to allow Stefan to worry, but she had no intention of frightening her grandmother. 'It is nothing,' she said and managed to produce a wavering smile for the Dowager. She avoided Stefan's eyes.

Stefan pressed her more tightly against his body. She could hear his heart thumping with an erratic pulse against her cheek. 'You must not move,' he said. 'It will increase the bleeding. Perhaps you would care to explain to me why you felt the need to fling yourself into the path of Franz Johann's bullet?'

Anna turned to look at her cousin, who was still sitting on the floor next to her, smiling amiably at the world and nursing his silver pistol.

'I thought he was going to kill you.'

'My darling, he has been trying to do that for a considerable period of time and with little success. There was no cause for you to risk your life. If you had not moved just when you did, I had every intention of knocking the weapon from his hand. He was not in perfect control of himself, you know, even when he aimed the weapon.'

She scarcely heard what he said after the opening

words. 'What did you call me?' she asked.

'I called you an idiot. Which is what you are. You have absolutely no sense of self-preservation.'

'It is therefore fortunate that she has you to take care of her, is it not?' remarked the Dowager, who had been watching this brief exchange with an interested eye. 'Ah! Thank goodness! Here is the doctor at last. Guards!'

The doctor rushed to examine the wounded Princess and the captain of the Dowager's personal bodyguard snapped to attention. 'Yes, Your Highness?'

'Take half your men and escort Prince Franz Johann to his suite of rooms. See that the doors are barred and that he is unable to leave his suite.'

'Yes, Your Highness.'

Four soldiers encouraged Franz Johann to get to his feet. He obeyed quite willingly, only proving recalcitrant when it became apparent that he was expected to abandon his place close beside Anna Teresa.

'I shall stay with Mama,' he said obstinately. 'Pretty Mama,' he remarked, absently stroking the blue skirts of Anna's dress.

The Dowager's face was taut with misery. 'Your Mama wants you to go to your room,' she said.

'No.' Franz Johann pouted stubbornly.

Anna Teresa motioned to the doctor, who was observing the exchange between his Grand Duke and the Dowager Grand Duchess with ill-concealed fascination. Anna swallowed the revulsion she felt and reached out to touch the back of Franz Johann's hand. '*I* want you to go to your room, Franz.' She swallowed again. 'Please be a good boy.'

His eyes filled with tears but he nevertheless scrambled to his feet in a painful parody of
youthful obedience. The troop of soldiers escorted
him from the room. Before he reached the huge
doors, he had started humming to himself, cheer-
fully singing the melody of a children's marching
song.

The music eventually faded into the distance.
There was a long silence in the Council Chamber.
At last, the Archbishop gestured to the Dowager
and they joined Stefan in an anxious group around
Anna Teresa.

'It is a surface flesh wound only,' the doctor
pronounced, confirming Stefan's diagnosis. 'Provided we take care that no infection sets in, Her
Highness should be fully recovered within two
weeks.'

The Dowager's firmly controlled features finally
relaxed into a smile. 'We shall have her carried to
her room immediately, so that you may commence
whatever preventative treatments are necessary.'

The Archbishop held up his hand in a signal of
protest. 'Your Highness, if the doctor would grant
us five minutes more of the Princess's time.
Perhaps, Prince Stefan, you would be able to place
Her Highness in a chair at the head of the Council
Chamber if you continued to support her with your
arm. I take it, doctor, that the Prince's prompt
action has stopped the bleeding?'

'Yes, yes. But I cannot approve any further
delays in treatment. Bullet wounds are not things to
be trifled with, you know. Infection is always a risk.
A grave risk.'

'The future security of Carthia also stands at risk,
Doctor.'

Anna Teresa struggled to sit up in Stefan's restraining arms. 'Of course I can stay for five minutes,' she said. Her mouth twisted in a grimace of pain that momentarily betrayed her. Quickly, Stefan moved his arm so that he was once again supporting the full weight of her body. With no apparent effort, he scooped her into his arms and deposited her, swiftly and gently, in the chair the Archbishop had indicated. He continued to stand beside her, ready to offer support if she needed it. The Dowager and Princess Luisa moved behind her chair.

The Archbishop cleared his throat. 'My lords, this is no time for delay or for long and elaborate speeches. The Grand Duke Franz Johann has demonstrated beyond reasonable doubt that he is not fit to govern our duchy. These are troubled times in Europe and in our country. I don't have to remind you that rebellions of one sort or another have occurred in virtually every state in Europe during the past eighteen months. This is not a moment to entrust the reins of government to a man who is no longer in full possession of his mental faculties. It is not even necessary to enter into a discussion of his previous wrong-doings. The facts of the current situation are clear.'

One of the oldest of the councillors rose to his feet. 'Our duchy has always been governed under the strict rule of hereditary succession. It has been the reason for our stability when so many principalities around us have suffered from upheavals and political disorders. What does it matter if Franz Johann is unfit to govern? We can leave him as a figurehead while this Council takes all the decisions. I say that this is not a moment to subject our country to all the dislocation of another change of ruler.'

'Franz Johann has not yet been crowned,' the Archbishop responded quickly, before any other councillors could voice their support. 'And we have here in this very room the legitimate and logical successor to Franz Johann. Prince Stefan is the second son of the late Count of Innesbad and the Dowager Countess. The Prince is married to Anna Teresa, daughter of the late Grand Duke of Carthia. Is it possible to imagine a more perfect couple to rule our country?'

There was a murmur of approval around the table, drowned out by the voice of the old councillor. 'But *is* Prince Stefan the legitimate successor?' he asked loudly. 'If nobody else dares to raise the question, then I am forced to speak out. I remember the events thirty years ago, even if the rest of you are too young!'

Anna Teresa could feel the rigidity of Stefan's body. Even though her thought processes were blurred by the throbbing pain in her shoulder, she could sense how he hated this public inquisition into the circumstances of his birth.

Calmly, the Archbishop displayed the sheaf of documents he held in his hand. 'It is better to bring this matter into the open,' he said. 'As you all know, for the last eight years of his life, the Count of Innesbad tried by every means in his power to show that he considered Prince Stefan his true son. He bitterly regretted the disagreements with his wife which led to Prince Stefan's banishment from Carthia. On his deathbed, he signed three separate statements testifying to Stefan's birth. In each document, he asserted that Stefan was to be con-

sidered in every way as his legitimate heir. After
Franz Johann, of course, who was . . . is . . . the
elder son. These documents have been approved
by His Holiness in Rome. There is no doubt, my
lords, that in law, Prince Stefan is the next heir to
the Dukedom of Carthia.'

'And in fact, as opposed to law?' queried the
Councillor.

'That, my friend, is a matter between the Count
and Countess of Innesbad and God. It is not for us
to decide, or even to speculate upon.'

'Prince Stefan has my support,' said the Dowager. 'My *full* support,' she added sternly.

'My lords,' said the Archbishop, spreading his
hands wide in appeal. 'Our country needs wise and
moderate leadership. You must accept the fact that
the peasantry will demand a parliament and if it is
not granted to them, they will fight for it until the
principle is won. Prince Stefan already has the
support of the peasants and the industrialists who
are building Carthia's first railway. He has the
support of Professor Muller's Democratic Party.
The Dowager has just offered him the support of
the Carthian Royal Family. Can we not offer him
our support also? This is a time to forget petty
squabbles, my lords, and to do what is best for our
country.'

The councillors rose to their feet. At first uncertainly, and then with greater enthusiasm, they
formed themselves into a single line and filed past
Stefan and Anna Teresa, kneeling to express their
loyalty to the new Grand Duke. Stefan shook
hands with each councillor, quietly helping the
older men back to their feet. Anna managed a smile
for each of them. As the last councillor bowed in

front of her, the smile wavered.

'I warned you, my lords!' the doctor exclaimed triumphantly. 'Do not blame me if her recovery is delayed by several weeks!'

'Anna?' Stefan said softly.

With a small sigh she turned towards him and collapsed into his arms as the world once again faded away.

It was the middle of the night when she awoke and knew that the worst pain was finally over. Her shoulder felt stiff and aching, but the intense pain was gone. She saw that a nurse sat close to her bed and a maid dozed in a chair by the bedroom door, but it was Stefan who drew her gaze.

He sat in an armchair placed close to the fireplace. Although it was late May, a small fire burned in the grate, no doubt in deference to her wounded state. Stefan stared unseeingly into the depths of the flames and their flickering glow outlined the planes and hollows of his face, casting its angles into even more severe lines than usual. She felt the familiar surge of love and longed to be able to reach out to touch his harsh features. It was exhilarating to know that she had the power to soothe those severe lines into an expression full of warmth and laughter.

'Stefan . . .' she said.

He heard her at once although her voice was very low, and he crossed to the bed with quick, eager strides. 'How are you feeling?' he asked, placing his cool fingers against her brow.

'Tired. Sleepy, and yet not wanting to sleep.'

He smiled at that. 'I had not thought you a woman of indecision.'

'I'm not. I've decided I would like to talk.'

Stefan handed her a glass of lemon barley water. 'Drink this first. You must be thirsty.'

Anna sipped gratefully at the cool drink while Stefan addressed the two servants. 'You may leave us now. I shall call you as soon as the Grand Duchess is ready to sleep.'

The servants curtsied respectfully and went quietly out of the room.

Once they were alone, Anna looked shyly at her husband. There were so many things she wanted to say that it seemed impossible to select any one of them. His face had returned to its old forbidding look and she had to remind herself that this look was merely a mask, protecting his inner sensitivities.

'Stefan . . .'

'Anna . . .'

They both spoke at once, then both fell silent.

'It was strange to hear you call me the *Grand Duchess*,' Anna said. 'I don't feel in the least bit like a Grand Duchess.'

His gaze softened into laughter. 'As long as nobody ever finds out how you chased across Europe clad only in a pair of my cast-off riding-breeches, I daresay you'll manage to fool all your would-be critics. You have a regal eye, my dear. In forty years time you will be as awe-inspiring as the Dowager.' He was silent for a minute, then said abruptly. 'I have to tell you something about Franz Johann.'

'Something has happened to Franz?'

'He is dead. Your grandmother's bodyguard escorted him to his rooms. He sat down at his desk and seemed to be absorbed in playing with his pistol. It was empty, and the guards saw no harm in the pursuit. I suspect that after a while they became bored and simply stopped watching him. There must have been a supply of poison in his desk, for when they next looked at him he was tossing pills into his mouth. He was dead before the first guard could reach his side.'

'I see.' Anna was surprised to find that the news of her cousin's death brought none of the fierce satisfaction she would have expected only a few days earlier. She had to remind herself that this was the man who had killed her parents and betrayed his heritage by overweening pride and warped ambition. She found that her strongest feeling was simply regret for the waste of a potentially brilliant mind.

'Yes, it is a tragic waste, is it not?' Stefan said.

'But I didn't say anything!'

'Your face says it all for you. However, speaking as the new Grand Duke of Carthia, I have to say that his death solves a knotty political problem. I had no desire to order the execution of my own half-brother, but a government is always more secure when there is no possible rallying point for the opposition.'

'Will there be opposition to your rule, do you suppose?'

'I hope so.' Stefan laughed a little wryly. 'If you remember, that's what the revolution was all about. The right to oppose the policies of the established government.'

'That's all very well,' Anna said tartly. 'But the right to opposition doesn't mean the right to armed rebellion against the lawful Grand Duke.'

'Your conversion to radicalism has not yet taken deep root, I perceive.'

'And your conversion to common sense has taken no roots at all,' she said crossly. 'A country must have some stability.'

'Wives, you know, are not expected to argue. They are expected to submit to their husband's political views.'

'That isn't a very democratic attitude. We should be equal partners in every way. Is that not the theory of democracy?'

He laughed softly. 'Did you not know that the most liberal theorists are always the worst autocrats in the privacy of their own homes? My poor darling, I'm afraid that you have acquired yourself a husband dedicated to the principle of male-dominated domestic tyranny.'

She allowed her hand to trail tantalisingly along the outline of his mouth. 'I shall have no influence upon your political decisions?'

'None,' he said inflexibly.

Her hand crept around the back of his neck and she pulled his head closer to her own. 'I was hoping to be present at future meetings of the Carthian Council,' she whispered.

'Certainly not.' There was a certain huskiness in Stefan's voice.

She sighed, and her lips brushed lightly against Stefan's mouth.

'Just the important meetings?' she murmured and pulled his lips tightly against her own.

Several minutes later, Stefan disentangled himself from her arms.

'I suppose—if you do not speak—there would be no harm in having you at occasional meetings of the Council.'

Anna Teresa smiled. 'Why don't you remove

your jacket and boots, Stefan, so that you could rest on the bed and give me some more lessons in your theories of democratic government?'

'Three weeks in your company, madam, may have addled my wits, but I'm not yet entirely devoid of sense. Besides, there is the problem of your shoulder. We must take care that you do not injure yourself even further.'

'I promise to lie very still,' she whispered. 'You would be amazed at how receptive I feel to further instruction in your theories of government. Especially if you remember to call me Anna.'

Stefan paused in the act of removing his jacket. He sat on the bed and took her uninjured hand, clasping it firmly between his own. 'Anna,' he said, abandoning all pretence of playfulness. 'At this moment, I scarcely remember what my theories of government are. Once in your arms, I shall undoubtedly forget whether or not Carthia even has a government. I love you to the edge of madness, you must know that by now. I once thought that I could have a good marriage with a woman I merely respected. Nowadays, I can no longer imagine what my life would be like without you. There are moments when I think that I couldn't feel this strongly about somebody unless they returned at least some of my love. There are other moments when I cannot think of a single reason why you should love me. Our marriage was created out of lies, and hatred and deceit. I want to change all that, Anna. Do you think we can?'

'I love you,' she said quietly. 'So I'm sure we can make our marriage whatever we want it to be. Sometimes it seems to me that I have loved you for ever . . . that I was just waiting for you to enter my life. Even when Franz Johann forced us to go through that ceremony in the cathedral, somehow I knew that the vows were real . . .'

He kissed her tenderly on the forehead, then, with increasing passion, hard on the lips.

'Damn that bullet wound!' he exclaimed when his exploring hands reached the doctor's thick pad of bandages.

Anna Teresa smiled serenely in the darkness. 'Patience, my lord Duke, is one of the first requirements of a democratic ruler.'

The Grand Duke of Carthia raised himself on one elbow and looked lovingly at his wife. 'Patience be damned!' he said and stopped all further argument with a kiss.